MW01277917

The Mansion

The Mansion

Álvaro Mutis

Translated by Beatriz Hausner

Ekstasis Editions

National Library of Canada Cataloguing in Publication

Mutis, Álvaro
   [La mansión de Araucaíma. English]
   The Mansion / Álvaro Mutis;
translated by Beatriz Hausner.

Translation of: La Mansión de Araucaíma.
ISBN 1-894800-20-6 (Softcover)
ISBN 1-894800-64-6 (Hardcover)

I.†Hausner, Beatriz. II.†Title. III. Title: Mansión de Araucaíma. English.

PS8593.I39D4313 2005   C843'.54   C2005-906278-3

The original Spanish edition, *La Mansión de Araucaíma* was published by
Editorial Seix Barral, S.A. Provenza, 219-Barcelona, Spain in 1978.

Published in 2005 by:

Ekstasis Editions Canada Ltd.   Ekstasis Editions
Box 8474, Main Postal Outlet   Box 571
Victoria, B.C. V8W 3S1   Banff, Alberta ToL oCo

THE CANADA COUNCIL | LE CONSEIL DES ARTS
FOR THE ARTS | DU CANADA
SINCE 1957 | DEPUIS 1957

BRITISH
COLUMBIA
ARTS COUNCIL
Supported by the Province of British Columbia

The Mansion has been published with the assistance of grants from the Canada
Council and the British Columbia Arts Board administered by the Cultural
Services Branch of British Columbia.

Printed in Canada.

Table of Contents

Introduction by Jim Christy   9

The Mansion of Araucaíma   15

OTHER TALES

    Before the Cock Crows   55

    The Last Face   81

    Sharaya   105

    The Strategist's Death   115

Translator's Afterword   139

Viens à ma volonté et je te donnerai tout ce que tu
voudras excepté mon âme et l'abreviation de ma vie

Gilles de Rais' *Letter to the Devil*

Introduction
by Jim Christy

Who is this man that Gabriel García Márquez calls "the second best writer in the world"? Winner of the Queen Sofía Award for poetry, the Cervantes Prize, the Prix Médicis, and the Neustadt Prize for Literature — Álvaro Mutis, nevertheless, remains practically unknown in North America.

Mutis was not caught up in the flood of Magic Realism that deposited so many Latin American writers, willy-nilly, on American and Canadian shores. On one hand, this is perplexing because Mutis's agent in Madrid had a lot to do with removing the flood gates; on the other, it is understandable because Mutis insists he is not a magic realist. His prose works — most of them featuring Maqroll, whom some, including myself, consider to be the great literary character of the age — seem to be told in a straightforward manner. And Magic Realism is anything — everything — but straightforward. Yet, Mutis's prose style is deceptive as will readily be discerned in these stories. The narrative rolls along, sometimes at breakneck pace, but the prose is redolent with intimations of more. More than he's telling.

Magic Realism is praised, and denigrated, for its baroque

excess, its suspension of time, the sheer improbability of events chronicled, and its folk whimsy. Back in the 1920s, Latin American authors began to gradually turn away from European models and to regard their own unique part of the world. They slowly acknowledged the mix of blood, the extremes of landscape, both geographical and political — a terrain where excrescence is the quotidian reality — and they forgot all about André Gide.

Then sometime in the Sixties, Latin American writers started to jack it up — like Nostradmus buying a crystal ball. Who needs it? Just to exist anywhere in those countries, in Mexico or Brazil, in Colombia or Panama is to experience the meaning of Magic Realism. As a friend of mine recently wrote on a post card, "We left Bogota after shootings at the school. On the way out of town I saw a dozen yellow chickens roosting in a tree with orange blossoms. An obese *mulatta* was asleep in a hammock."

Mutis has never had to jack anything up, to call on folk whimsy or turn literary tricks. He is among the most learned of men, but no *litterateur*. He has lived largely, travelled widely and read extensively.

"I never earned my living from writing," he has said. "I scribbled my poems in hotel rooms before meetings or at night while having a drink at the bar."

Mutis was born in Colombia in 1923 and educated in Belgium where his father, a diplomat, was posted. Returning to his native country at the age of eighteen, he worked for Colombian National Radio, reading the news and commenting on classical music. When he was twenty, he worked in public relations for LANSA, the Colombian airline that developed into Avianca. For five years he was head of public relations for Standard Oil in Latin America, but Mutis didn't write news releases or speeches for executives. He travelled on tankers, went with prospectors and geologists into the jungle and was the press liaison in times of disaster. It was Mutis who dealt with the families of victims of explosions.

And then there was the trouble. He was found guilty of defrauding Standard Oil of Colombia and spent fifteen months in Lecumberri, the notorious prison in Mexico City.

"I managed a sum of money at Standard Oil, and this money was for social programs and charities. Well, I had some friends who were in trouble, trouble with the military dictatorship of Colombia, and I used the money to help them. It is true that I also spent some of the money to throw a few parties."

As William Burroughs might put it, "Wouldn't you?"

Mutis left Colombia during the investigation and went to Mexico City where he was soon picked up by Interpol. In prison he had no privileges. His diary of those months, published only in Spanish, bolsters translator Beatriz Hausner's contention that many of the characters in *The Mansion* are based on people he encountered in that hole known as the Black Palace.

Those characters recorded in the diary are worthy of Honoré de Balzac, Feodor Dostoevsky, Henri Charrière, and Mutis's real literary hero, Charles Dickens.

In 1959, after a change of government in Mexico, Mutis was released from prison, and the next year the charges against him were annulled. He began working for Columbia Pictures as commercial director for Latin America. "I travelled throughout Central and South America, and all this time, whenever I could, I wrote."

Mutis made his literary name as a poet. He has been called the voice of his generation, and he was, in more ways than one. At about the same time that he began working for Columbia Pictures, Mutis was hired to do the Spanish voice-over narration for the original television series *The Untouchables*, which was wildly popular in Latin America.

Beginning when he was eighteen years old, Mutis had by his

side — on boats, in the jungle, in prison, at his writing desk — a companion, his great creation, the character, Maqroll.

We never learn whether that's his first name or his last; we don't know where he's from, how old he is or his nationality. He speaks several languages, including English with a vague Levantine accent. His nickname is the "*gaviero*", acquired back in the last days of sailing ships when he practically lived in the crows' nest: the lookout.

"I was eighteen and I started writing about things I knew nothing about — could, at my age, know nothing about. So I invented an alter ego."

His first book of poems, published in 1948, features Maqroll. The book that won the Queen Sofía Award for the best book of poetry published in the Spanish language in 1977 was *Summa de Maqroll el Gaviero.*

When, however, Mutis turned to adult fiction for the first time — he had published a children's book based on the legend of the Pied Piper of Hamlin — Maqroll does not appear. Yet Maqroll hides between the lines and his shadow, as much as any person encountered in Lecumberri, falls across these pages.

I cannot recall another slim volume of stories with such breadth of achievement. Here Mutis offers historical fiction, religious parable and intense character study in styles that remind one, by turns, of Borges, Machado de Assis, Antoine de St. Exupéry and Louis Ferdinand Céline. He employs disassociative time, the old, recently-discovered-bundle-of-manuscripts ruse and something that may best be described as "jungle noir". His people are always musing and lucubrating, eating, working, making love, and seeming to defy fate while being resigned to it.

The Mansion has all the elements and is a precursor to the masterful prose Mutis would employ in the seven Maqroll novels soon to come.

But most importantly it is what Mutis doesn't say — the atmosphere he creates, the silence around the notes — that makes the reader aware of the *more* that is always beyond our grasp. There are times in his work when Mutis sounds like a grizzled tenor in an opera at the edge of the world, backed by a choir of dissolute angels, singing a threnody to the great beyond.

Yes, his work is death-haunted, as is only the greatest writing, but there is nothing morbid in it. Rather, it celebrates that recognition of death which sanctifies and enhances life.

Personally, I think Gabriel García Márquez got the order reversed.

The Mansion of Araucaíma

A Gothic Tale of the Tropics

For Newton Freitas

The Keeper

He had once been a soldier of fortune, a mercenary for hire by governments and people of questionable character. He had been a regular at bars where men at arms volunteered for colonial wars — thus becoming the oppressors of young uneducated nations struggling under the illusion that theirs was a fight for liberation — when, in fact, the only noticeable change achieved was a slight fluctuation of the rates in noisy stock exchange floors. He was missing one arm and was fluent in five languages. He smelled of bittersweet jungle plants which give out an aroma of freshly cut wounded bark.

He spoke to no one when he arrived and settled in one of the rooms surrounding the inner courtyard. Once there, he noisily unloaded his regulation backpack and, following a most personal order, laid out his belongings around his sleeping bag. He lit his pipe and began to smoke in silence. A few days later, while he bathed in the river, someone noticed that he had a number and a carefully drawn woman's sex tattooed under his right armpit. Everyone feared him, with the exception of the owner, who was indifferent to him, and the friar, who felt a rather austere fondness towards him. His manner was abrupt, exact and measured, at once gentlemanly and old-fashioned.

From the moment he arrived he was entrusted with tasks

which gave him control of the movements of the other residents in the mansion. He was in charge of the keys to all the rooms, as well as stables and farming installations. Everyone was forced to go to him whenever a tool was needed, or fruit had to be delivered to market. He was not known to have ever denied anyone a request, yet no one would take anything without informing him beforehand, not even the owner. Undeniable force and authority emanated from his missing arm, from the tone of his voice and the rather rigid manner of his gaze when people addressed him.

He remained on the sidelines as the events unfolded, and no one could say with certainty whether he participated in the preliminary stages of the tragedy. His name was Paul. He washed his clothes in the river with an air of resignation and habit-acquired ease that could move any woman. His long leisure hours were spent playing military airs on his harmonica. It was painful to watch him play with one hand while he helped himself along with the stump of the other, trying to draw marches out of the precarious instrument.

The Owner

H ad someone pointed out obesity as one of his physical attributes, few would have remembered it as a distinguishing trait. He was, nonetheless, colossal. There was something flabby about him — soft, not fat, as though he fed himself on substances altogether foreign to man's everyday diet.

He claimed to have inherited the mansion from his mother, but it soon became apparent that it had fallen into his hands by virtue of legal scheming whose integrity few could risk attesting to. His name was Graciliano, but everyone knew him as Don Graci. He had been a pederast of some renown in his youth and had, on occasion, been thrown out of cinemas and other public places for making passes at adolescent boys. Age, however, had distanced him completely from such practices, and to assuage his occasional urges, he would, during his baths, have recourse to masturbation with the help of a mentholated shaving soap on which he stocked up generously during his now infrequent trips into town.

Don Graci's participation in the events was of capital importance. It was he who conceived the sacrifice and to him were due the ceremonial details that preceded and followed it. His maxims, which ruled the order of life in the house, had been written on the walls of the spacious living quarters and went as follows:

"Silence is like pain, it propitiates meditation, moves to

order and prolongs desire."

"Defecate daintily, for time spent at it doesn't count, yet when you add it up, you build on eternity."

"Looking, like the whore's mirror, is a three-faced sin. In one face you see truth, in the second doubt, and in the third, the certainty of having erred."

"Raise your voice in the soft silence of the night when everything quiets down as we wait for dawn. Then, raise your voice again and bemoan the misery of the world and its creatures, but let no one know of your weeping, nor anyone decipher the meaning of your laments."

"One leaf equals vice, two equal a tree, the sum of all leaves barely equal a woman."

"Don't measure your words. Measure, rather, the moist skin of your intestines. Don't measure your actions; measure instead, the rabbit's urine."

"Stay back, allow the fire to delicately consume the work of man. Stay with the water. Stay with the wine. Stay with the hunger of the condor."

"If you enter this house, don't leave. If you leave this house, don't come back. If you walk through this house, don't think. If you live in this house, don't sow your prayers."

"All desire is the sum of the voids through which our soul escapes on its way to outer space. Consume yourself in yourself."

Time had erased other maxims, and the owner's own hesitating memory had made their reconstruction impossible, a fact which did not seem to concern his guests in the least. Their pompous style and artificial conciseness were perfectly suited to the plush gestures of that robust column of flesh whose hands moved as though arranging silk fabrics inside a wardrobe.

He had large, dark and watery eyes which must have once made his listeners blush, but now produced in them the fear of having to witness an abusive, somehow sickly suspension of time. He was vastly cultured, though no one ever heard him quote an author. Nor did anyone ever see him hold a book in his hands. His knowledge was the fruit of a miserable childhood spent in the refuge of his scholarly father's books and in the dark library of a Jesuit school.

We have touched on Don Graci's participation in the events. It must be pointed out, however, that in some ways he was the sum of all the events. More accurately, it was he who gave origin and meaning to those events. Since he didn't avoid his role, but simply chose to ignore it, what eventually took place assumed the proportions of a bothersome infamy, the result of license both incomprehensible and inevitable. We will elaborate more on this matter later, though no longer in the same terms nor from the same point of view.

Don Graci never took baths alone. He bathed twice a day, once in the morning and again at night before bedtime. He chose his bathing partners but made no demands of them. Nor did he speak to them during those long ablutions which, on occasion, though these were now few and far between, gave off an intense menthol-like scent.

The Pilot

The pilot's hands were sweaty. He had piloted planes for a small airline founded by friends dating back to his days in the Air Force Academy. He worked there until a large corporation took over the small airline. He looked for work with other airlines but was always politely turned down because of his looks and personality. He turned up at the hacienda while flying the light aircraft Don Graci had hired to fumigate the neatly-planted orange and lemon trees that lined his property on the shores of the Cocora River, when the plantation was threatened by plague. He had barely finished his job one stormy evening, when the small plane was struck by lightning and caught fire. The pilot stayed behind at the mansion drawing to himself neither the rejection nor the good will of anyone else. It was La Machiche who brought about his staying permanently. She chose him for one of those fleeting affairs of hers, no doubt drawn by the little mustache he sported over that well-drawn, fleshy mouth so typical of weak men. He had a narrow forehead. His dark, straight and abundant hair gave him an air of virility which soon proved entirely deceptive. It wasn't as though he suffered from impotence, though it was obvious that he had a marked tendency towards an indifferent frigidity, which soon proved offensive to La Machiche and alienated her from him for good.

He roamed the house with a vague smile, as though he blamed himself for taking up the space no one offered him. In the evenings he would help the friar with the hacienda's bookkeeping, adding up the figures in round, silly handwriting, typical of someone schooled by nuns. Wherever he went, he carried with him the flyer's manual from the company he had worked for as flight captain. He would go over it meticulously every night before going to sleep. He wore a threadbare lead-blue uniform and a dirty cap bearing several Air Force badges. His name was Camilo, and he had bad breath.

His participation in the tragedy was not only of prime importance, it was conscious and carefully meditated for reasons to be seen, or guessed. It was La Machiche who plotted the long invisible intrigue against the pilot and turned him into the principal player, after the victim. So great was his desire for self-destruction, that his own weakness forced him to assume the most delicate and decisive part of the drama.

He was the author of the lyrics that the victim learned to sing to the melody of a song much in vogue at the time and which went like this, more or less:

> *You don't have to be king of the world*
> *to find a woman*
> *on a summer afternoon.*
> *There are quiet waters near the beach*
> *where the sun builds transparent tents.*
> *Every morning I go there*
> *and wait for a different girl.*
> *You don't have to be king of the world,*
> *you don't have to be anybody in life,*
> *you just have to wait and let*
> *the clear air caress your brow.*

Aside from the questionable quality of the intense refrain, what irritated everyone most was the expression of delicious vanity on the pilot's face every time the victim sang it, as though it were the most beautiful song he had ever heard. What she saw in the lyrics when she sang them with such emotional fervour was unknown to the friar and Don Graci, the only ones learned in such matters. Maybe everyone's destiny was at stake in that song. It was difficult to say.

La Machiche

A ripe and luscious creature, La Machiche. Her skin was white, she had ample sagging breasts, generous hips and buttocks. Her eyes were dark, her face was defined by a strong jaw, high cheekbones and an avid mouth: It was the type of face those illustrators who chronicled the gallant Parisian lifestyle of the past century would have favoured. At once terrible and docile, she was called La Machiche for whatever erotic talents she may have cultivated in her prime. She lived at the back of the mansion. Every time she made her way down the corridors of the house, her huge black mane, with its soupçon of gray hairs, announced her presence, as though preceding the eruption of her abundantly offered flesh.

La Machiche possessed a natural intelligence, like most of her gender, but also a spontaneous talent for evil, a tenderness ready to burst, to protect, to caress and avert pain and misfortune. Goodness came furiously to her. Her cunning machinations brewed slowly, only to erupt in complicated, noisy disputes which she later resolved by means of accelerated cooing in one unmade bed or another.

La Machiche's participation was definitive. More than jealousy, it was an exaggerated premonition of evil and decay wrought by time — had the situation prolonged itself — which prompted her to think up the idea of the sacrifice. This, with the consent and even wise advice of the owner.

La Machiche was in charge of all the housework. Her preference as far as men were concerned was not known. The giant servant was the only person one could imagine as having had a secret and permanent bond with La Machiche, although no facts ever surfaced to prove such a liaison. She was afraid of the friar, felt contempt for the pilot, got along well with the keeper and would talk at length with the owner.

Don Graci was particularly patient with her. Whenever he invited her to join him in his ablutions, the others stood around the large bathtub watching La Machiche in all her splendid nakedness. Her skin was of a remarkable whiteness, and despite her age, there was a milky freshness about her. The three plump folds on her belly were not so much the sign of improbable past pregnancies, as of prolonged and much exploited lust.

Her hoarse laughter filled the room every time she partook of the owner's baths. He liked to pour water on her from his considerable height, using a huge container shaped like a conch shell. There was no contact between them other than a respectful acquiescence on her part and a vague fondness on his. At most, what could happen was that at the culmination of their baths together, Don Graci, in the altogether apocryphal tone of a preacher, would call her "The Great Whore of Nineveh." From each of these baths La Machiche emerged with a new suitor to whom she devoted her pampering and care, all the while attending to the others with the provident efficiency of a mother.

La Machiche went around barefoot and wore a long flowered dress which had a frilly neckline and reached below her knees. She wore no embellishments. She gave off a sour scent tinged with the aroma of benjamin, which followed her as she made her way around the house.

La Machiche's Dream

She walked into a large hospital, a modern clinic built on the shores of a clear pond of tranquil waters. She crossed the main door and proceeded along wide, silent corridors painted in a flat creamy colour, lit by soft filtered lamps which emitted a slight drone. She walked through a door which read "Entrance" and came up to an examination room. A doctor dressed as a surgeon approached her as he took off the mask covering his mouth: "We hired you to pull out the weeds and lichens that are growing in the operating room, in the laboratories and in some of the corridors. It's not a heavy job, but we require your complete dedication. We can't allow these weeds, all these plants to keep growing everywhere," he said, pointing at the cracks in the floor. He led her into an intensely lit operating room. Inside, the nickel-plated instruments gleamed, reflecting the milky lights which buzzed constantly. Imperceptible lichens grew in the cracks between the tiles. She began meticulously pulling out the plants, yet as she progressed with her task, she realized that it was all a trap. The plants kept growing persistently, continuously. She thought that supper time would never come, that the moment she stopped working, the plants would easily gain ground. All of a sudden, she understood that there was no one supervising her for the simple reason that it was an impossible task, a useless confrontation with

27

time: those short, woolly and warm leaves kept appearing every-where, with tireless animal insistence. She began to cry, overcome by a gentle and secret grief, a yearning she had kept deep inside herself and could not remember having felt while awake.

"How do you expect me to make the trip?" the pilot kept saying as he watched her from a large terrace bathed in a morn-ing light so bright that it hurt her eyes. "How do you expect me to move from here when everyone knows I'm a good for noth-ing?" The pilot smiled sweetly. He was wearing an impeccable flight captain's uniform as well as large sunglasses to protect his eyes. The sunglasses made him look at once elegant and strange. He kept smiling at her with noticeable complicity, until she real-ized that she was baring her breasts every time she bent down. She tried in vain to cover herself, but the weight of her bosom kept opening the soft nylon robe she had been given to wear. It was a nurse's gown. "Do you want me to help you?" he asked her from above, speaking in a protective tone which she felt was complete-ly uncalled for. "But you don't know how to do this," she replied, trying not to hurt his feelings. "You never knew how to do it with me, and you don't know how to do it with her either." "I did it once, which means I am able to do it," was his answer. He turned his back to her as he greeted someone who had appeared at the other end of the terrace, someone of great importance, invested with immense authority and on whom depended everyone's des-tiny.

She was combing her hair before a mirror which shifted position with the movement of her arms, making it very difficult for her to look at herself. During those brief moments she was able to see herself properly, she tried to fix her hair by gathering all the strands into one long braid which she rolled up on top of her head. She realized that this was an old-fashioned way of doing up her hair, that in so doing, she was trying to reconstruct a cer-tain period of her youth, an atmosphere now faded, one she could not identify with her past, which appeared confused, filled with an inexplicable sadness without solace. The doctor who had hired her came in. He embraced her from behind, pulling her toward him as he spoke to her softly: "You did that very well. Come now; don't cry. You look so lovely like that. Come, come," and he drew her to him with a warmth which aroused her and returned her untouched to the happiness of years past.

The Friar

He claimed that he had been the confessor of the beloved Pope, now deceased. No one would have believed him, had it not been for a letter he received one day which flaunted the papal tiara, two crossed keys underneath. He put the letter away without reading it, nor showing any interest in its contents. Everyone called him "the friar." No one ever found out what his real name was. He was alone in refusing to share Don Graci's baths, a fact the latter learned to accept with a certain irony at first and surprising resignation in the end.

He was handsome. His appearance seemed to have remained fixed somewhere between forty-five and sixty, a stage in a man's life when he always looks the same age — maintaining the same face, the same body. He was aware of his physical poise, but did not seem particularly satisfied with it and never used it to subject anyone to the dull and somewhat disorderly state of his affairs.

In a way, his part in the events was marginal, yet of capital importance. When the time came, he heard the victim's confession and proceeded to reprimand the executioners with fiery oratory but not much conviction. He was the author of the Morning Prayer which the inhabitants of the house adopted, reciting it always at the same time, wherever dawn overtook them. It went like this:

O Lord, make order in the sorry state of my faculties.
Make the day pass over the bitter shadows which burden me.
Give me, O Ever Kind One, the key to the meaning of my
days, for I am lost in the world of dreams, there where you can
not reign, nor is your presence found.
O Lord! Bestow upon me a flower for consolation.
Find me shelter on the lap of a woman who can replace my
mother, prolong her in the fullness of her bosom.
O fortunate one, free me from man's bitter awakening, that
I may grow numb before the holy innocence of mules.
Lord, you who understand the uselessness of my labour on
this earth, do not make me partake of it. Instead guard it until
my final hour. Do not grant it to me during my laborious wake
fulness.

Lord: weapon against all wounds
flag against all defeats
tool against our sorrows
nickname for fools
father of lemurs
pus of the banished
eye of the storm,
step of cowards,
door of the bashful.
Wake me up, O Lord!
Wake me up, O Lord!
Wake me up, O Lord!
Hear me, O Lord!

Some diligent scribe had tried to copy the prayer on the walls under the owner's maxims, with the consent of some and the furious disapproval of the owner.

"My words need to be written down because they are lies, and only when it is written down does a lie gain validity as truth," he said. "We all know the prayer by heart so there is no need to record it anywhere."

The friar was the only one who owned weapons. He had a Colt pistol and a diver's dagger. He cleaned them constantly and looked after them with compulsive zeal. He did not use them, nor did he rid himself of them when it would have been opportune to do so.

Such was the friar.

The Friar's Dream

He was walking along a corridor. He crossed a doorway and found himself, again, going along the same corridor, but for a few details that made it different. He thought he had dreamed the previous corridor and that this one was indeed the real one. He found himself crossing a doorway yet again, going into another corridor with new details which set it apart from the previous one, making him think that he had also dreamt the former one, that this was the real one. In this manner he kept successively crossing new doors that led him into corridors, each of which seemed to him as he went along to be the only existing one. He surfaced briefly into wakefulness and had this thought: "This could be another way of praying the rosary."

The Girl

The girl was the victim. She was seventeen and had arrived at the mansion on a bicycle one afternoon. The first person to see and welcome her into the house was the keeper. Her name was Angela.

She had been playing the lead role in a film being shot at the hotel of a large summer resort. Its shareholders were keen on promoting the sale of lots for a development next to the resort. The film showed a young blonde, her hair blowing in the breeze, with an air of Alice in Wonderland about her, riding her bicycle up and down the more interesting spots, strolling along the avenues that bordered the coffee plantations. It showed her bathing bashfully in a river whose shores were dotted with old-fashioned park benches and garden furniture.

By the time the shooting was over, the only ones left at the hotel were the photographer, his two children, and a few production people. The girl had stayed behind as well, and devoted herself to riding her bicycle and visiting all the places which had piqued her curiosity and were not included in the script. One of the sites was the large house of an estate where citrus grew and pheasants and geese were raised. It was the mansion.

At first glance she looked like a rather conventional movie actress: blonde, tall, well-built, with long lithe legs, a narrow waist and small athletic buttocks. Firm breasts, a long neck always tilting to the left in a rather conventional manner, completed the image of the girl, perfectly suited for her role in that short film.

Only her eyes, her glance didn't fit the whole. They conveyed a tired feline expression, always on guard. There was something slightly unhealthy and vaguely tragic floating in those faded green eyes that gazed fixedly, leaving those around her feeling ignored, mere outsiders to a world sometimes visible through their aqueous, quiet transparency.

Her father, a famous lawyer, had committed suicide one day, for no apparent reason, though it was later learned that he was sick with cancer of the throat. He had concealed his illness until the pain began to betray him. Her mother was one of those society women who, without belonging to a family with pedigree, become members of the upper class by grace of their appearance and by virtue of certain routine good manners which conceal any probable vulgarity or crass upbringing. Once she became a widow, the small fortune she had inherited slipped through her fingers with a swiftness typical of beauties of her generation. The girl had started working as a model and then began her film career with modest roles in musical comedies. She was engaged to a medical student. She had been initiated into sex by one of the studio electricians for whom she had felt one of those disorderly and loveless passions which brings a person closer to the one who first reveals pleasures as yet unknown and distant to us. She enjoyed making love but felt strange when she climaxed, as though detached from herself. There were times when she became so unhinged, she could see herself moaning, breathing noisily with pleasure, all the while feeling a tired and complete indifference toward that convulsed being before her.

The keeper, hardened though he was by his life as a mercenary familiar with death and violence, felt immediately captivated by the eyes of the visitor. He let her in, forgetting the strict instructions imparted by Don Graci where outsiders were concerned, ignoring the tacit understanding which ruled the mansion: the group was now complete and no stranger would ever be brought into the fold. The breaking of this balance was perhaps the final and secret reason for the misfortunes that soon befell the mansion.

The Girl's Dream

She was riding her bicycle through the lemon groves that bordered the river. She knew that this was impossible in real life, but in the dream she found no difficulty at all in doing so. The bicycle rolled softly over the dried leaves and the moist plantation soil. The air brushed her face with refreshing, invigorating force. She felt her entire body invaded by a freshness that at times gave her the unpleasant sensation of life beyond the grave. She entered an abandoned church with a vast resounding nave which she quickly crossed on her bicycle. She stopped before a brightly lit altar. The owner, dressed in the ample feminine dress of a Byzantine Madonna, was represented as a life-size statue. It was surrounded by a great number of votive lamps, their little flames swaying softly as if induced by an other-worldly smile. "It's the Virgin of Hope," a skinny little old black man explained, his hair white and curly like that of sheep. He was the servant's grandfather and addressed her with a reproachful tone making her feel ashamed and anguished. "She will forgive your sins and those of my grandson. Light her a candle."

The Servant

ristóbal, a huge Haitian who spoke awkwardly and moved about with the elastic, silent gait of a primate, was the servant at the mansion. He shopped for groceries at a modern super-market in the development next to the hotel and would go down to sell oranges and lemons to wholesalers he had previously arranged to meet at the train station. The business brought Don Graci ample profit.

Cristóbal, sweet and cautious, a large black man the owner had brought back with him from one of his adventures many years before, was said to have complied, in days now forgotten, with certain whims of Don Graci's with the peaceful indifference with which his race fulfils the urgencies of sex. But even though Don Graci had done without the intimate favours of the black man, the same did not apply when it came to his always efficient service where the house was concerned. La Machiche inherited him in her search for that final, complete satisfaction so difficult to find for someone like her, after a lifetime of licentiousness. She felt no affection for Cristóbal, and he did not show any passion for her either. They united with furious anxiety every two months or so. They would lock themselves in Cristóbal's room, which was beside the friar's, to the latter's despair and sleepless irritation. La Machiche's long sighs and Cristóbal's furious snoring followed each other in an endless series of episodes, punctuated by laughter and sobs of pleasure.

Cristóbal had been a practitioner of Macumba in his native land, but now practiced his own personal rites with unorthodox modifications which involved the suppression of animal sacrifices in favour of long alchemies with plants. On given days the smell of macerated herbs coming from his room would permeate the whole house, prompting Don Graci to protest: "Tell that son of a bitch to quit that witchcraft of his, or we'll all drown in the damned incense."

At a given point, Cristóbal's participation in the events was providential. His sharp, natural instinct led him to the girl with accurate intuition of her true personality. He knew to ignore the young woman's absent eyes, and when he took her to bed she did not fall into convulsed spasms as was her habit, but flung herself completely into the whirlwind of her senses, satisfied at last as she emerged from the test feeling calm and purified. Therein, however, lay her undoing, the premonition of her subsequent sacrifice.

The servant was a good friend of the friar's, with whom he spoke in French tinged with a slight accent from the islands. He got along best with the pilot, however, and would welcome him with the protective attitude of an older brother, which the former aviator used to secure for himself certain privileges at meal time, as well as additional pampering, like hot water to shave with and a change of sheets every morning. The influence Cristóbal exerted over Don Graci was that of someone who had at one point known how to keep in check the robust owner's desires. Toward the keeper, Cristóbal showed the pent-up resentment his race feels, born of seeing the first white soldier setting foot on African soil in military uniform. They never addressed one another directly, nor did they make outward signs of their mutual distaste, except on occasion, when a brusque, cutting order from the soldier was met with a sarcastic "oui monsieur le para."

On Corpus Thursday Cristóbal used to prepare a delicious spicy chicken broth, and the best pieces always went to the pilot and La Machiche. As he served the meal on that day, he would begin a long psalmody of which a few paragraphs still remain. He would say for example:

> *Alaba bemba*
> *in the name of Orocuá*
> *the chicken is now cooked.*
> *For the one who wants to taste it*
> *Cristóbal prepares it.*
> *He serves it but doesn't eat it.*
> *He eats it but he doesn't taste it*
> *because this man killed it*
> *killed it in the morning*
> *so today's sun the chicken will not see.*
> *Borucue's Aracua*
> *dead soul of the great Bondo.*
> *May the Bunde forgive me.*

The string of verses went on indefatigably. For the rest of the day Cristóbal would be sad, irritable and would sigh with childish melancholy.

He was left-handed.

The Mansion

At first sight the building looked no different than the other estates in that coffee-growing region. However, upon closer inspection, it became obvious that it was much bigger, proportionately larger, unjustified and gratuitous in its rather intimidating vastness.

There were two floors. A continuous corridor on the upper floor surrounded each one of the three courtyards which followed one another toward the back. The last courtyard merged with the orchard of orange and lemon trees. The bedrooms were on the upper floor; on the first, were offices, tool and storage rooms. In the stone-paved courtyards the faintest noise from someone remained floating in the air, while the water murmured happily in the pools where the fruit was washed and the coffee was pulped. These were the only perceptible sounds one heard when entering the cool, nostalgic atmosphere of the courtyards.

There were no flowers. The owner hated them. Their scent gave him an unpleasant rash on both the palms of his hands and on his thighs.

The rooms around the first courtyard were closed up, with the exception of the one occupied by the keeper who, as mentioned earlier, had spread his belongings on the floor upon arriving — there they had remained, in that transitory and precarious

41

order typical of soldiers. The other rooms, five in all, were used for storing old furniture and rusty machinery whose purpose was unknown to the current inhabitants of the house, as well as large cupboards full of ledger books and old magazines bound in impersonal, monotonous blue cloth.

La Machiche and the pilot lived in the rooms opposite the second courtyard. It was there that the girl sought refuge on her first night at the mansion under conditions that will promptly be revealed. Don Graci, the servant and the friar lived in the last courtyard. The owner's room, the largest of them all, was made up of two rooms whose dividing wall had been torn down. A big brass bed rose from the centre of that large space and was surrounded by chairs in a great variety of styles and conditions. In a corner, at the back, was the bathtub which rested on four sphinx claws carefully carved in the most abominable fin-de-siècle style. Two paintings decorated the place. One was a somewhat naive rendition of a sugar cane plantation on fire. Beasts of exaggerated proportions were fleeing the flames in horror, an infernal glow in their pupils. A man and a woman, naked and terrified, fled among the animals. The other painting portrayed a Madonna, almost gothic in style, holding a child who gazed at her with an obvious, mature resentment, completely alien to the serene expression on the mother's face.

The mansion rose at the confluence of two fast-flowing rivers which crossed a valley planted with orange, lemon and coffee trees. The surrounding mountains were tall and of a deep blue colour and kept the valley in shadow, as if in secret intimacy, as if guarded by large trees whose spare foliage was crowned by the ever present purple flowers that provided shade to the coffee plantations.

A railroad, built many years earlier, provided access to the valley through one of the gorges, where white water fell in noisy torrents. Later, having regretted drafting something so altogether irrelevant to practical use, the engineers had diverted the railway away from the valley. The two bridges were all that remained and bore witness to their original plans. The bridges were still used for transporting people and animals. They had roofs made of zinc sheeting so that every time droves of mules from the hacienda crossed the bridge, the floor echoed with mournful monotony.

"Araucaíma" was the name of the hacienda. It was thus indicated in lilac letters on the faded tablet with gold borders placed over the main gateway to the first courtyard of the mansion. The origin of the name was unknown and resembled no other name used to identify places or rivers in that region. It could have been something Don Graci had fancied, fruit of reveries born of who-knows-what memory of his distant youth in other lands.

The Events

The keeper took the young woman to the second courtyard of the house and called down to La Machiche to come and take care of her. The girl wanted to wash her face and touch up her makeup before going on with her stroll, but one could read in her eyes a curiosity to look around, to get to know from up close the place she was so drawn to.

The two women came face to face in the lower corridor. La Machiche had noticed the girl waiting next to the keeper on the paved courtyard. The girl, in turn, had perceived the opulent humanity of that sour, distrustful woman who studied her, not without envy, conscious of the aggressive youthfulness emanating from that young body like an invisible, ever-present halo.

"This girl wants to know where the washroom is," explained the keeper unceremoniously as he left without waiting for a reply.

"Come with me," signaled La Machiche, and the girl followed her along the second floor gallery until they reached a small room. A washbasin on a tripod served as the room's main fixture. In the back, behind a dirty pink curtain, was the toilet and up on high, the water tank, eaten away by moss and rust. "You can wash your face here, and if you need anything else, the toilet is behind the curtain. Close the door first if you're planning to use it." La

Machiche left the girl there, surrounded by the buzzing mosquitoes and the room's humid silence.

After washing, the girl went into the corridor and came face to face with the pilot, who was carrying some papers with a hurried air about him. He was taken by surprise by the sudden appearance of the girl and greeted her with that welcoming, facile smile which came to his face almost without his willing it. After the keeper and La Machiche's welcome, the pilot's smile felt like the very epitome of kindness to the girl. They chatted for a while leaning on the banister that gave on to the great silence of the courtyard, growing darker under the evening shadows.

The pilot invited the girl to stay at the mansion that night, as darkness was upon them and the road back to the hotel would be impassable by bicycle. She accepted with the lightness of someone who yields to fate blindly, with the faith of a sacrificial animal.

It is not easy to reconstruct the events step by step, nor to call forth the days the girl lived at the mansion. What is certain is that she became part of the household and began to knit the net that would pull them all, without their realizing it, into the disaster. She did this unawares, like someone who is part of a complicated blind mechanism which governs each hour of one's life.

For two nights she slept in the same room as La Machiche. She then resolved to go and sleep with the pilot, whose easy cordiality attracted her and whose stories of the countries he had visited she found extremely seductive. When, despite the endless caresses that left her in a state of tired hysterical arousal, the pilot was unable to possess her, she left him and went to sleep alone in a room in the second courtyard next to the one the friar used as a study. It wasn't long before the two established a friendship based on sincere affection and an unspoken, yet deep understanding of the flesh. The friar would undress her in his study, and they would make love on the dilapidated leather armchairs or on an enormous library table covered with papers and dusty magazines.

The friar loved the girl's frank, direct disposition which kept their relationship on the fringes of passion. She, in turn, was seduced by the serene and solid firmness with which the friar avoided any trait of the childishness, banality or pure and simple weakness, typical of relationships between men and women. They made love furiously and stayed up talking afterward in friendly and serene company.

It was the owner, Don Graci, who, with the envy of the invert and the gratuitous maliciousness of the obese, secretly incited the servant to seduce the girl and take her away from the friar. In fact, Cristóbal was waiting for her one day when she went for a swim in one of the canals that crossed the orange groves. After long, mournful purring, he convinced her to give herself to him. On that day the girl had a taste of that ancient, impatient African lust made up of long swooning and violent curses. From then on, like a sleepwalker, she went to their encounters in the orchard and gave herself to the servant with hopeless tameness. She told the friar what had happened and, though he continued being her friend, he never again took her to his study. He acted thus, not for fear or prudence, but rather because of a secret sense of order, a resolute intuition for balance which placed him beyond the chaos hinting at annihilation and death.

In the beginning La Machiche pretended not to know about the girl's new liaisons, and said nothing. She still slept with Cristóbal when she needed to. It was at this point that she began to feel a growing desire to once again seduce the keeper, who had left her years before and had never since paid any attention to her. As long as La Machiche was interested in the soldier, things went smoothly. But as soon as the mercenary reprimanded the servant, the calm was broken. Their dislike for one another was obvious.

One night, when the keeper was expecting her for one of their rendezvous, La Machiche stood him up. Through an untimely comment of Don Graci's at the breakfast table the next day, the keeper found out that she had slept with the servant. Opportunities abounded during the day for the two men to have a run-in, and as soon as the soldier gave the servant one of his contemptuous cutting orders, Cristóbal flew into a rage and threw himself on the keeper who responded with two skillful blows. The servant fell to the ground. The keeper left him there and went on his way as if nothing had happened. Later that night he told La Machiche that he wanted nothing to do with her, that he could no longer stand the servant's stench on her, that that white wharf-matron's body of hers no longer awakened in him any desire whatsoever. La Machiche ruminated on her anger and disappointment for days, until she found someone on whom to vent it with impunity. She fixed her gaze on the girl, inwardly blaming her for her own failure with the keeper. She decided to take her revenge on the young woman.

The first step was to win her trust, and she found not the least difficulty in doing this. Angela lived in a state of constant arousal. Her failure with the pilot, her truncated relationship with the friar and the violent and sporadic episodes with the servant had left her prey to an inexhaustible, ever-present lust which suggested itself in every object, in all the events of everyday life. La Machiche caught on to the girl's state of mind. With kind words and a complicity which can exist only between women, she invited the girl to share her room again. Delighted, the girl accepted.

One day, before going to sleep, while they were comparing the details and shapes of their bodies, La Machiche began caressing the girl's breasts distractedly. Unable to conceal her growing excitement, the girl became silent and let the experienced whore continue. La Machiche began to kiss her, leading her to bed and,

47

once there, discreetly but surely showed her the way to satisfy her desire. The ceremony repeated itself several nights in a row, and Angela discovered the feverish world of love between women.

Thanks to La Machiche's own remarks, it was not long before Don Graci found out about the affair. The owner began inviting the two women to join him in his baths, without the presence of the other inhabitants of the mansion. Don Graci presided over the women's lovemaking and, when the opportunity presented itself, he enjoyed making suggestions, thus sharing in the girl's spasms from the neutrality granted him by age. As the days passed, the girl became more aggressively fond of La Machiche, allowing the older woman's own wayward instincts to lead her toward their chaotic dead end.

As soon as La Machiche knew that Angela was under her complete control, that the girl could satisfy her desires only through her, she delivered the final blow. She did it with the proven serenity of someone who disposes of another person's life, with the calm detachment of a beast.

One night, the girl went up to La Machiche's bed as she leafed through a magazine. Angela began to kiss her large naked legs while La Machiche read distractedly, or pretended to do so. She remained indifferent to the girl's caresses until Angela perceived her friend's changed attitude.

"Are you tired?" she asked with a hint of complaint in her voice.

"Yes, I am tired," answered La Machiche bluntly.

"Just tired, or tired of me?" inquired the girl with the foolish candour of those who are in love, those who fling themselves into the deepest abysses by virtue of their own words.

"To tell the truth, dear, I'm tired of all this," La Machiche began to explain in a neutral voice that painfully penetrated all of Angela's senses. "You interested me a little at first, and when Don

Graci invited us to take baths with him, I had no choice but to accept. You know that he supports us all, and I'd rather not go against his wishes. But I'm a woman for men, dear. I need a man — I was made for men, to be their enjoyment. Women don't interest me, they bore me as friends and they bore me in bed, especially you, who are so green, so inexperienced still. Plus, Don Graci no longer calls us to his baths. He too must have gotten bored of always seeing us do the same thing. We are going to leave this thing alone, little girl. Now go back to your bed and sleep. What I need is a man, a male that smells and moans like a man, not a little girl who squeals like a sickly cat. Go on now. Get some sleep."

At first Angela assumed it was just a sick joke, but the tone of that strapping woman's voice was so consistent with the truth that she quickly understood that La Machiche was speaking in earnest. She was filled with fear at the thought of never again being together and making love. She rejected the whole idea as impossible, but it kept coming back to her, time after time, imposing itself like an irrevocable reality. She went back to her own bed like a sleepwalker and began to cry persistently, tirelessly, desolately. La Machiche was lulled to sleep by Angela's crying, comforted by the sweet taste of revenge.

The next morning, the keeper went into the tool shed and found Angela's body hanging from one of the beams. She had hanged herself at dawn by tying a coarse rope around her neck, climbing on a chair and kicking it away with her feet.

Funeral

They took the body to Don Graci's room and laid it on the floor. The servant and the keeper went to the river's edge to dig the grave. The owner asked the friar about the events, and the latter brought him up to date on all the details. The friar told him that the previous night, the girl had knocked on his door asking for his help, begging him to hear her confession. The poor thing was in a sad state of inner turmoil and felt that the world had suddenly and definitely collapsed around her.

La Machiche was not present at the friar's account and went and locked herself in her room in a surly mood. The pilot also left the room before the friar began telling his story. He said he needed to go over some accounts and asked the friar for the keys to his room where the receipts he needed were kept. He displayed a disturbing serenity in view of the girl's fate.

When the friar had finished his account, Don Graci commented: "I don't know who's to blame for all this, but it could mean a lot of trouble for us; you will see. From the very beginning I was opposed to having this girl living here, but since nobody heeds what I say and you all invariably end up doing whatever you want, we will now have to bear the consequences. We must fix this woman up before putting her to rest." Don Graci was referring to the need to cover Angela's naked body which, togeth-

50

er with the first signs of rigidity, showed her feminine attributes with a certain ostentatious ripeness. Her breasts had become visibly developed under La Machiche's care and her swollen sex offered itself with an obviousness barely concealed by her pubic hair.

The friar and Don Graci washed the corpse with an infusion of orange leaves which, according to the owner, slowed down the decomposition process. They wrapped it in a sheet. They had almost completed the task when two shots were heard coming from the second courtyard. A violent struggle was heard, followed by a sharp blow and the ensuing warmth of the evening silence. The friar and Don Graci rushed over and saw from the corridor that the keeper was holding the servant against the ground. Beside him, lying on the stone floor, La Machiche agonized with two large wounds in her chest. Her abundant dark blood poured out of those wounds with each death rattle. Further down lay the pilot, his skull grotesquely shattered. The friar ran over to help La Machiche, who kept repeating, between the gurgling and contortions of pain: "It had to be that faggot... It had to be..." Don Graci went over to the keeper and ordered him to let go of the servant, who was writhing on the ground with his face against the stones. The soldier obeyed Don Graci's orders and freed Cristóbal, who gently walked away.

"We had just finished digging the grave when we heard the shots," said the mercenary. "The pilot shot La Machiche and had the friar's gun in his hand. Cristóbal went at him, without giving him time for anything. One blow of the shovel brought him down. Once he was on the ground, Cristóbal went on hitting him, until I managed to immobilize him. It was like he'd gone mad."

The friar took care of everything. The keeper helped him take the bodies of the two women to a grave they had dug by the edge of the river and buried them together. La Machiche had died cursing the pilot furiously, begging them not to let her die.

The pilot's body was taken to the furnaces of the sugar mill. When Don Graci went to the servant to ask him to light the burners, he found him in his room on his knees facing the bed, praying before a portrait of Victor Manuel III. He was praying in his dialect, sobbing deeply. Still weeping, he went to the furnaces and, while he stoked the fire, kept quietly murmuring: "Machiche…, ma petite Machiche…, ma gandamblée, Machiche ma gurimbo…" A tenuous blue smoke rose in the clear afternoon sky signaling the voracious work of the flames. A little pile of ashes and his captain's cap hanging in the gallery were all that was left of the pilot.

That same night, Don Graci abandoned the mansion with the servant, who left with him, carrying his suitcases. Two days later the keeper prepared his backpack and left on the bicycle Angela had brought with her. The friar stayed behind a few days longer. In leaving, he closed all the rooms and the entrance gate. The mansion was left abandoned, as the winds blown in by the great rains whistled down the corridors and whirled in the courtyards.

OTHER TALES

Before the Cock Crows

The first few houses of the city came into view. They went on arguing, interrupted only by long pauses which served to replenish the reserves of rancour stored inside each one of the men. The Master finally lost his patience and ordered them to stop bickering, whereupon they all fell into a frightened silence inside the vehicle.

"That's enough!" he said with sudden energy in his voice, leaving no room for answers or disobedience.

They had started arguing the moment they got on that rickety bus, with rustic wooden seats, which had picked them up by the shores of the lake. It had to do with a hotel bill still owing from the last time they had been preaching in the area. When the bus picked them up, the one who seemed to be their leader and whose eyes betrayed a feverish inner tension attenuated by a honey-eyed sweetness, signaled them to stop yelling at each other, obviously afraid that the other passengers in the bus would take notice of the matter. But the stubbornness of the oldest of the twelve, who went around dressed like one of the fishermen of the harbour, together with the indefatigable and furious eloquence of the one responsible for the funds, who wore a dirty raincoat buttoned up to the neck over his equally grimy clothes, were stronger than the explosive authority of their leader, who now looked nervous-

55

ly around at the other passengers, trying to smile and thus lessen the importance of the whole affair.

They were all overcome with emotion when they got off at the bus terminal, situated at one end of the market.

It wasn't the first time they visited the place. They enjoyed a certain popularity among the people in the market, the same kind of popularity they enjoyed at the docks, in the fish stores and among the women who lived in the launderers' quarter.

They headed in that direction in silence, led by a young man dressed as a mechanic who had recently joined them. He was related to the owner of a guest house with one of those laundries on the first floor, a typical feature both of the neighbourhood and of the city in general. A crowd of followers began gathering around the group — and some, the more daring ones, surrounded the Master, possessed by a fervour and respect so extreme as to make them rip pieces, sometimes an entire pocket, off his threadbare corduroy jacket. One man had even tried to grab the greasy silk scarf, printed with blue and white boats in all shapes and sizes, that he wore tied around his neck. The Master defended himself clumsily while he scolded the one in the raincoat:

"I don't reproach you," he said, "for your venality or the meanness of your lies, meant to hide the fruit of your stealing. You know all too well that the alms we collect belong to all of us equally, that the reason we trust you with them is because we know the esteem you hold for money, because we know how good you are at managing it. Do you really think I don't know where all our common funds end up? I could, if I so chose, tell you how to double and triple the yield of your investments, obtained as they are through our preaching. But it is written that you will be the one to carry the weight of infamy, and there is nothing I can do to deliver you from this, even if I so wished. Like me, you go headlong to your destiny, and it would be easier to stop the flow of water in a river with one's hands, than to twist the course of our lives and modify the way they will end."

He listened, half with irony, half with fear, accustomed by now to the Master's language, spattered as it was with those somewhat naive images and obscure expressions.

The treasurer held a silent grudge against the Master which had never completely manifested itself and which he would set free by way of slander and tricks. The whole situation had come to a head the day before when the Master had caught him trying to hike up the skirt of one of the girls at the guest house, and though she showed no marked resistance, it seems the Master had feigned exaggerated repugnance at it all.

When they arrived at the hotel, some of the disciples dispersed the beggars, the sick and the fanatics who had followed them. As they went up the stairs they were greeted with warm enthusiasm by two women, one of whose round, uncomfortable belly surprised the younger man and made the Master grimace as only he could, with a face full of disgust and pitiful reproach. Pregnant women infuriated him; they made him irritable and confused, unbearable even to his closest disciples. The only available three rooms were shared by all of them. While they showered and changed into clean clothes, the oldest went up to the room next to the terrace where the Master was going to sleep, normally used to hang laundry to dry, to inform him of certain rumours going around concerning his apostolic mission.

"Things have changed considerably since we were here last, Sir. The new mayor is a lackey of the shipping companies. Groups of extremists are being rounded up by the police, and the jails are full. The unions are in the hands of leaders who've sold out to big business. They are the ones who hire gunmen to instill terror in the slums and the dockyards. Gatherings are closely watched, and strikes have been banned. Despite all this, the stevedores and customs officers are preparing a work stoppage and are arming themselves. I think that, this once, we should go by unnoticed — limit ourselves to collecting funds among our trusted friends and, once we have enough money, go on our way, just leave without preaching or stirring things up, as people are quite worked up by the agitators on both sides."

His advice couldn't have been more untimely; it was greeted with a reaction entirely contrary to the one the old fisherman had sought. The pent-up irritation from the quarrel in the bus, the exhaustion from the travelling, plus the unexpected pregnancy of that girl, all these exploded with violence.

"The way you see things is worthy only of you and your puerile senility. You will never learn to discern when a situation is ripe for use in our favour and in favour of our faith. You, like the rest of the pusillanimous bunch who follow me out of laziness, seem to believe that our mission consists of preaching to the simple-minded, of performing miracles before the gullible, of living off their wretched alms, of taking advantage of their hospitality and eating at their tables. A soft bed, a good meal and easy women, it seems that's about all you aspire to! Swine! That's what you are, living in the filth you came from. And," he went on vociferating, "when, by express means and divine order of the heavens, the time comes for us to sacrifice ourselves, to prove the fecund truth of our doctrine with our blood, you run away like terrified rats! Fool, you will readily see the harvest we'll reap today! There's much to be gained from the disorder that reigns in the city! The success of our cause depends on us! We'll throw ourselves into the struggle and will light a bonfire that will burn forever and ever. The time we've been waiting for has come! We are ripe for our sacrifice, for showing the perpetual wonder of our example! Get up, you rascal! Get up and call the others! We'll gather the people and will go down to the docks to preach, now that they are busiest!"

Only age and familiarity with the sea make possible an intuition like the one the old man had at that moment. Clear before him, like a capsule of the future, the scenes of the end, wrought by the arbitrary moods of the leader, appeared to him. His intuition also told him that nothing more could be done now. It was necessary to restore each event to its original force and attempt to rescue what little living matter old men certain of their destiny avidly pursue.

Without saying a word, he helped the Master get dressed. As he was tying the scarf with the boat designs around his neck, he looked directly at the Master and read, etched in his face, the whole tragedy as it was going to unfold.

They went downstairs. The others were already waiting at the door. The youngest was talking to a man who had approached the group, inquiring about room rates. The fisherman and the one with the scarf burst in, cutting the conversation off abruptly.

"Let's go down to the port!" exclaimed the Master. "Those thirsty and hungry for justice are waiting for us!"

The stranger saw them leaving, but slipped away so quickly that he had disappeared by the time the others turned around to look for him. A shiver ran down the old man's back. The group started walking, followed at a little distance by the one in the raincoat who had lagged behind to settle some accounts with the owner of the hotel. He was now trying to catch up to the others with a quick, firm step, seemingly devoid of any muscular effort. The group was made up of people of all classes and backgrounds. Two of the men had worked at the lake's canning factory but had quit their jobs in the middle of the peach harvest, even though the pay was good. There was the train conductor who let them ride the train for free when there were just five of them, and who got off the train and joined the group after a long, three-day trip.

During that journey the Master had rushed out to preach in the cars, causing great chaos in the train. The conductor was forced to stop the train twice — once to allow for the hysterical wailing of the women to subside and, the second time, to wait out the confessions of those who, suddenly struck by guilt, began to loudly proclaim their sins. A travel agent had joined the group, as did a man who traded currency at the border. There was also the young man who sold stuffed birds, the kind of taxidermy used for decorating the sitting rooms of the rich bourgeoisie and the waiting rooms of elegant brothels. They were subsequently joined by a sign painter whom the enlightened leader had scolded for practicing the abominable sin of advertising. Left behind on the railroad tracks lay the cans of paint and the brushes he had been using to paint a huge, smooth woman's underarm which promoted the excellent results of a shaving cream. His family had assumed him dead for years, and this gave way to a story concerning his resurrection at the hands of the Master. Two young fishermen, as well as a mechanic who specialized in motorboat engine repairs and was the youngest in the group, had followed the old fisherman we all know by now. The last two were cabinet makers by trade and distinguished themselves by their circumspection and shyness. They were apparently related to the leader and gave the impression of knowing something they feared uttering out loud by giving into excessive talking.

The one in the raincoat had at some point rented them a sound system and, seeing that they were getting such good results with their sermons, had decided to join them, secretly drawn both by the role that awaited him in the story, and by the opportunity this presented for getting away without paying debts he had incurred in the city after trying his hand at various business deals without success.

Despite their diverse backgrounds and professions and the

reasons that drove them to follow him, they all had absolute faith in the man's miraculous powers and in the goodness of his doctrine. Furthermore, despite the Master's fearful moodiness, a certain serene and solid sense of justice and of human brotherhood determined his actions, making their faith in him unshakable.

When they arrived at the docks, two large ships which had docked at noon were being unloaded of their cargo of crystal. They came from distant countries of ice and mist and were painted white, except for their chimneys, which sported large yellow and blue rhombi. The stevedores and crane machinists on duty watched the delicate task with growing attention. Their bosses had announced that each broken piece would be deducted from the workers' pay. The group watched as the heavy crates that were being unloaded travelled through the air, guided with miraculous dexterity by the large cranes. A dust of fine straw mixed with white sand fell out of the crates into the eyes of those standing below, making them cry incessantly. The strong, salty smell of the sea blended with the fresh aroma of the pine crates and chimney smoke, evocative of those sad skies of northern industrial cities. To make the operation possible in one shift, the women had brought down lunch boxes and baskets with snacks for the men. When they saw the Master and his disciples, they surrounded him with reverence and stood there listening. Here and there a stranger or one of the guards got close to listen.

What the Master said wasn't particularly virulent, nor were his words more fiery than on other occasions. But the ground was ready to be sown with the seeds of violence, and very soon the growing attention of the dock workers and machinists added itself to the women's agitation. By the time the disciples realized that something out of the ordinary was going on, the cranes had long since stopped operating, and a siren had sounded announcing a brief dinner break. The old fisherman and the travel agent were the first to understand that something serious was about to happen. The police and the strangers who had joined the faithful earlier were nowhere to be seen. From the now silent dock, the lonely voice of one man rose like a tall jet of water, pointing to the golden afternoon sun.

Suddenly, a howl — half moan, half contained scream — was heard over the Master's voice. Everyone turned in the direction of the lament. An enormous crate swayed in midair, at the will of the cool late afternoon breeze. The ropes groaned under the weight of the crystal ware. A little cloud of straw flew off the pine planks, fluttering in the breeze toward the sea.

The Master stopped preaching and was watching the vast expanse of ocean which disappeared into the horizon, rocking to and fro, like an endless cradle.

The paramilitary squads burst in suddenly and the sirens of the harbour police closing off the intersections, began to sound. The first tear gas canisters exploded. They had barely woken up from their momentary reverie, when the rifle butts started to ruthlessly beat down on men and women alike, forcing them to roll on the ground spitting blood and crying in horror.

The police, contented with dispersing the curious who had stopped to listen to the Master, instead vented their fury on the nucleus of disciples and on their leader. First they beat them with rifle butts, then forced the group into a van that drove through streets and squares, never once turning off the siren until they had arrived at a police station carefully chosen for this case. It was located in a residential neighbourhood far from the city centre. It was the kind of place where, though rarely, a son gone astray would end up after a night of heavy drinking, where they would take a servant girl after she let her man into her employer's house for a night together and some petty thieving.

It was one of those neighbourhoods preferred by bankers, by

successful businessmen and influential public servants — the type of people who prefer spending their vacations by the ocean, who enjoy a good game of golf on Saturdays and are members of clubs and charities.

At this point, it was a matter of letting the entire responsibility of the disturbances of the last few days fall squarely on the shoulders of the Master and his friends. In this manner, they could also justify the repressive but extremely effective measures they had taken to put down the revolt, while at the same time preventing any further attempt at the use of violence on the part of the dock workers, the unions and potential sympathizers among factory workers. The officer normally in charge had been replaced that day by someone with specific orders to act in this fashion.

An improvised but efficient group of collaborators acted as his consultants. The police van went through a wide door and stopped at the end of the building's inner courtyard. The first one to stumble out limping was the former train conductor, whose eye had been closed shut by a truncheon blow. The others came out of the van in silence, a silence broken only by the deaf, wounded animal moans that a man lets out when his flesh hurts and he is tormented by fear. They entered the interrogation room in single file. Under the harsh light of bare bulbs they made the sorriest, most unusual sight imaginable. They were shaking from the pain of the blows and their wounds. The humiliating anguish which the police inflict on their victims through their implacable actions had taken complete hold of them, depriving them of even the simplest ability to reason. One by one they gave out their personal information. The Master's turn came. Blood was flowing from a wound on his forehead, and his paralyzed left arm was grotesquely twisted as a result of the numerous fractures caused by rifle butt blows. He gave his name, his age, and when the officer — a small, obese man, whose manner, though meticulous and

seemingly kind, barely concealed his cruel and cold nature —
asked him what his address was, his answer was:

"I don't have a fixed address. My mission is to spread the
truth, to sow it down any road, wherever people suffer from
injustice and pain."

"Let's avoid the sermons," the functionary answered. "Get to
the point."

"Whoever wastes his time with me, earns time in eternity,"
he answered without flinching.

"Yes…, yes… I know already. Very well then, you are
charged on counts of subversion of the public order, of conspir-
acy against state security, of rioting, of criminal association, the
illegal practice of medicine, fraud and pimping. In the warrant for
your arrest we have declarations from witnesses which prove each
one of these charges. Do you have anything to declare?"

"He who weaves a lie, weaves his own shroud and shall lose
his soul," the accused answered once again with complete serenity.

"If you have something to declare against the accusations
brought forth by the Ministry of Public Affairs, say so, and please
don't speak in parables or metaphors anymore. It's too late for
that now and you will be risking your life and that of your accom-
plices," the officer warned with impatience.

"If I have failed in some way, then I am the guilty one. These
men followed me because of my counsel and the fame of my
deeds and are, therefore, innocent. Don't lessen the worth of your
judgment any further through useless sacrifices."

"That is for me to decide and not you! Lock them up!" the
officer ordered.

The guards took them into the courtyard. They crossed the
deep warmth of a night that was stirred by sleepy, slow moving
clouds travelling over the ocean in search of daybreak in other

lands. Everyone felt as though under the spell of the promise of an impossible happiness, attainable only in the open spaces high above them, beyond the vanity and insignificance of their affairs. The old fisherman had lagged behind looking at the moon, when suddenly, rushing through his blood and disturbed by pain and shame, he felt the drunken freedom of the sea he had enjoyed during those endless years spent travelling and fishing for sperm whales and tuna whose mad, nomadic whims had ruled his sea-faring ways. A blow from a rifle butt on his kidneys brought him back to the present.

"Let's get going, grandpa, let's get going — this is no time to be gazing at the stars," and with one push he fell on the wet cement. Thin threads of warm, sticky blood now flowed from several points, blood whose touch only added to the horror undermining his most essential energies. He dragged himself over to the wall and lay down. Once his eyes got used to the darkness of the cell, he was able to make out the Master's outline before him, his face wrapped in a net of dry blood.

A long time passed before either of them spoke. From the very first day of their meeting at the docks, the two had arrived at a tacit pact which excluded from their relationship the many pompous, doctrinaire formulas the Master used in order to distance himself from the rest of his disciples. His friendship with the old man took place at a deeper level; a larger truth flowed through the words of their conversations, as if each had reserved a certain space, an isolated domain where the other exercised no right at all.

"What now, Master?" the old man finally asked.

"Things have begun to fall into place and there is nothing we can do but wait for the miracle."

"But we will die, Sir, and everything will be lost forever, and no one will be free of misery, and injustice will fortify its foundations against all."

"It will be quite the opposite. My sacrifice will provide you with the tools to sow the words of salvation all through the world, and you will be the foundation of my temple."

"But, my Lord, we are alone, and no one knows about our imprisonment — and when they find out, it will be through the mouths of those who have arrested and humiliated us. Those same people will make sure their version suits their interests, and we will be portrayed as charlatans and criminals. We must try to leave this place as best we can, admit to some of the charges, then seek better luck elsewhere. Otherwise we will be lost, and with us, your words, your message."

"Your faith fails you because of the pain of your flesh and the fear gnawing at your heart. They can do nothing against us. Not even your weakness can prevail against us nor against yourself. I entrust you with my doctrine, with my truth and yet, before the cock crows you will have denied me three times."

"You are delirious, my Lord, fear is also working in your body making you see us as weaker than we really are."

"The cock will say. Now let me be with my father."

Peter became silent. Before long, a deep dream filled with anguish and silent screams of horror forced him to lean his head on the shoulder of his companion whose gaze seemed lost in a nameless eternity, the source of his miracles and preaching.

The old man woke up with a start. They were shouting out his name. The guards were shouting it, and his friends were repeating it like a hushed chorus. Half-asleep and dazed, he got up and walked out into the freshness of the dawn now washing the courtyard with a milky substance made of the cool breeze from the sea and the dew that had condensed over the sleeping city. He took a deep breath. He yearned to live, to remain standing on this earth, to enjoy those enduring simple things which make the world the only place left for people to live in. Something grabbed at his throat and a deep, almost joyful sob rose in him. They took him before the officer once more. The latter calmly shuffled some papers, took out the ones he was looking for and began the interrogation.

"So you have a fishing license. There aren't any damaging records in your file. In fact, I see that you have two mentions with the coast guard for having twice helped your mates in danger. It's clear that you're not of the same sort as the others. You're not a drifter without a trade, a charlatan taking advantage of the credulity of others. What urged you to seek such company? Who forced you to follow them?"

"No one forced me, sir. Some have been friends of mine for years and, like me, are peaceful people and upright citizens."

"And what do you say about the others, the ones you didn't know before? You don't think the same of them, do you? Answer me!"

"I don't know about the others, sir. I couldn't say, really. I've known them for such a short time."

"And yet you live with them, you conspire with them, you cheat old widows with those so-called resurrections and other infamous lies."

"They are good men, sir. As far as the miracles go, there are documents to…"

"Yes, I'm well aware of how these documents come about. Stop pretending you're an idiot and answer me! The leader, is he a friend of yours?"

"No, sir. I met him just a few months ago. He stayed at my house, and I lent him my boat to go and preach to the fishermen who were coming in from the sea. I didn't know him before that, sir."

"Aha! So you went and followed him without even knowing

him?"

"I don't have my nets anymore, sir. I rented them out to some fishermen at the lake, and rather than staying at home, well…"

"You took to the road like some old peddler! Well, well… You don't seem so wise for an old man after all! And, what do you think of the so-called Master? Who is he, and where does he come from? What's he trying to do with all this agitation? Come, answer me! You are a citizen of this town, people know you as a serious, honest man, your fellow workers respect you… Are you going to dirty your name, the profession you've served for so many years at the expense of your life, of all those bitter efforts, just to help a man whose parents and birthplace you don't even know?"

"No sir. I intend to go back to my job. I merely wanted to get to know the ways of the mainland. I spent my entire life at sea and had never gone inland. I tried it, and now I will go back to my work."

"Fine. Let's see if it isn't too late to repent. Come, sign here and we'll leave you alone; you'll go back to your boat and your fishing nets."

The old man examined the writing. It was a long, complicated sequence of legal formulas that concealed something quite simple — his retraction from any complicity or sharing of ideas with the Master, as well as a hidden but conclusive confession to the effect that he had followed the Master without any faith in his doctrine, that more than anything else it was curiosity and adventure which had driven him on. He signed in silence and was taken to a small bedroom where two officers were sleeping. It reeked of cheap liquor and the sour penetrating stench of sweat. He was given a blanket and they pointed to a small metal cot with a worn-out mattress which had a stain in the middle, from so much use.

He lay down and fell asleep.

He dreamt that he was giving water to some horses that gazed at him with big, sad and watery eyes before lowering their heads to a pail he could barely lift off the ground. Standing next to a cliff in the distance, her strong legs spread apart for balance, his mother held a big white candle and made it sway as a way of sending signals into the solitary sleeping sea. Each time they lowered their heads to drink, the horses would mutter, in an incomprehensible language, something shameful in relation to the woman and her gestures. Troubled though he was, he tried to smile, not wanting to admit that he was aware of what was being said by those animals whose neighing was getting louder and louder. The sounds of rifle butts hitting the courtyard tiles woke him up. A group of officers was getting ready for their morning meal.

He went out and wandered through the corridors without anyone paying any attention to him. He tried several times and without success, to figure out where they had been locked up the night before. He got lost in a labyrinth of hallways and doors that opened and closed continuously to give way to guards and assistants who came and went in a hurry with a worried air about them. The time that had elapsed since they had been on the bus travelling to the city along the lake shore had been erased from his mind. A bothersome uneasiness prevented him from keeping still, as though he had something urgent to do and could not think of what it was.

Sometime toward noon, one of the doors that led to the back of the courtyard opened. He heard a groan, like the ones bulls let out when they are being castrated, mixed with sounds of women laughing, most probably drunk. The door closed locking out both moans and laughter. The old man suddenly came back to the reality of the previous night and the events that had brought him there. He remembered the Master and his inseparable scarf. He remembered the man in the raincoat. He hadn't arrived there with the rest of them. And he hadn't been at the port either. Or maybe he had — in the beginning. Yes, he had been there at first, but then vanished. And the young mechanic with relatives of dubious character, and the man who sold stuffed birds and his tireless chatter. A sharp pain made him lower his head. He had denied them. He had denied the Master. He had made him seem like a stranger he followed for no reason other than to find some distraction, to pass the time. The truth was that the Master had introduced him to his mother when they had gone into the mountains that summer. Together they had visited his father about some carpentry work that needed doing on the fisherman's boat, and the two older men had talked for a long time about their youth and the hardships they had endured when they were learning their trade. And there was more. It was Peter who had insisted on following them, because in the beginning the Master had seemed somewhat reluctant to accept him. He considered Peter to be at the end of his life and the task required of him beyond his strength and agility of mind. He was the only one the Master considered a personal friend. The Master felt not only a special liking for him but a certain respect for the maturity his age bestowed upon him. And he had denied him — just as the Master had predicted, with a kind of clairvoyance.

His sad meditations were abruptly interrupted when two women burst into the courtyard through the door he had heard the commotion coming from. They were dressed in crumpled but expensive evening gowns and still showed signs of drunkenness. The policeman who was with them was still smiling from whatever had gone on behind those doors.

"I am the fountain of life and eternal resurrection!" shouted the youngest of the women, who had a masculine, athletic air about her, at once vicious and hysterical. "This guy sure has guts! At first I thought he was coming on to me or something… I didn't realize till I saw him from up close. Ha, ha, ha. Those fish hooks will make anyone rise up from the dead! Let your little doll bring you back to life, honey. Just let me bring you back to life, baby. Let's play, I said. You should have seen the face he made. Ha…ha…ha… As if a bug had stung him!"

"And the kid. What did you think of the kid? The mechanic…" said the second one, a tall, dark-haired woman whose frigidity could be hinted at behind the cruelty of her large, motionless lips and the calculated, languid glance of her big, dead eyes. "Did you notice how he tried to console the other one from inside his own cell? I think he is one of them. Did you notice how he cried for his Master? His dear Master! That's what they must call each other now. They come up with new names every day!"

They strutted past him with the long martial sway of their hips and legs, without as much as a glance, leaving behind a stale, sour smell, a mixture of expensive perfume and vomit. "Like mares in the paddock before the race," he thought, "and just like mares, useless, easily aroused, capricious, harmful and insolent." The women crossed the courtyard and left through the centre doors. A guard walked them to the street and came back, buoyed by the affected familiarity the girls had treated him with, wanting to insinuate that he had done a lot more with them than his comrades could be led to believe. "All for a cheap thrill, for some crazy jaded attitude they mistake for sophistication," the old man kept thinking. Yes, they must have been talking about the Master.

About him and the young man. They must have had some fun at their expense. That's what the guffawing and the moaning had been all about. A painful fear tore at his gut, rose and knotted itself in his throat. And the others? The guards went by him without paying much attention and did not respond to his shy attempts at finding anything out. Finally one of them, perhaps in less of a rush than the others or maybe just nicer than the rest, stopped:

"What do you want, grandpa? What did you lose around here?"

"Do you know anything about the Master? Where are his disciples?"

"Don't tell me you belong to that band of wretched men. You seem respectable enough and your white hair just doesn't fit that kind of clowning."

"No, of course I have nothing to do with them. I was just curious... There's so much talk about the whole thing..."

"Well, they simply laid all the blame on their leader. The others left at dawn, except for the youngest, who insists on staying behind to help him through his final hours. He has confessed to a few things. Enough so he can be accused of having conspired against the security of the State, of fraud and other worse crimes. He'll be executed this afternoon. I think he's a bit touched; it's hard to understand what he's saying. Do you want to see him?"

"No," answered the frightened old man. "I was just curious... Thank you. Thank you very much."

"But, what are you doing here anyway?" asked the guard, suddenly intrigued by the old man's presence at an hour when the courtyard is accessible only to surveillance personnel and people in custody for special reasons.

"Me?" stammered the poor man, even more frightened than before. "Nothing..., nothing..., just paying a fine, you know, for fishing in waters that belong to the Naval Base... Rules, you know, are very tough, it's nothing serious."

"Very well then," answered the guard, who had calmed down by now. "I hope you get the matter sorted out soon, pop. As you can see, this is no place for people like you. Those whores made such a racket last night! They had their minds set on getting it on with the prophet and told him whatever came into their heads till they had to be removed by force. It's not the kind of show your gray hair should have to witness. Well, I hope things get sorted out quickly. Good-bye."

"Thank you," answered Peter. "Thank you very much. Good-bye."

He remained motionless, deep in thought, feeling as though a great shame once again invaded his being. But this time, the sensation of a gentle letting go of his inner springs began to overpower his guilt feelings. Memories of his life at sea, of his family, of his daily routine at the docks began to surface, forming a solid crust on which shame slid away, no longer hurting those deep, secret zones which now retreated into peaceful darkness.

Noon had come and gone and at around one o'clock two guards, whose faces showed confusion and fatigue, came out of a door at the back and gestured for him to get closer. The expression on their faces was that of someone who has committed something shameful and forbidden. The old man's white hair made them feel even sadder, and they barely managed to utter an unsure "come with us." This, in a low but harsh voice which awakened in him the very same terror he had felt the night before. They walked down a narrow corridor with iron doors painted white. At the back, a small intensely lit room stood out — it looked like a doctor's consulting room. There were a few chairs, a dark red leather couch, typical of a doctor's office. A few surgical instruments, oxygen and anaesthetic cylinders confirmed the infirmary look of the place. A strong smell of disinfectant, mixed with the sweetish smell of fresh blood, floated in the air. He went in, dazzled by the intense light of the lamps. The guards pushed him gently forward by the shoulders.

"He wants to speak to you. The officer gave him permission.

There's nothing left do with him. You can talk all you want. We'll come to get you in due time. Now hurry, get in here." And they left, the sound of their boots echoing in the hallway.

The old man suddenly understood. An instinctive urge to follow the guards, to flee, to avoid looking at that form tied to a white metallic tripod, tottering grotesquely, spitting blood, moaning like a wounded child, pushed him back toward the door which had safely shut by then, thanks to a powerful spring. Confused, filled with shame and suddenly feeling the fire of pity invading him, burning his throat, he got closer until his face came against the labourious breathing coming out of orifices that connected what had once been a mouth and a nose and which now served to insufflate a bit of air into the victim's macerated flesh. He gazed at him in silence, while tears of tenderness began to stream down his weathered seaman's face. He felt the reverberations of all the wounds and humiliations palpitating in the victim, as though a peculiar, special kind of reflex were at work within him.

The Master was naked, falling forward, his face now deformed by punches from a knuckle duster that had erased every trace of a human profile. One of his eyes, emptied from its orbit, hung like a whitish bloodied tatter. His other eye moved incessantly, crazed inside its skinless socket. They had worked on the fracture until they had dislocated his arm completely. On the other arm were horrible burns: acid dripped from his fingernails, bubbling as it touched the floor, spreading into black stains. The legs had been brutally opened, revealing his monstrously swollen testicles from whose skin they had hung a multitude of fishhooks, the kind fishermen normally use to catch trout. Some had brightly coloured feathers, others a delicate insect with vibrant elytra, and others were nickel-plated spoons that swirled amid the glitter. The rest of the hooks were of indeterminate, colourful shapes.

A thread went through all the hooks joining them to a rope that hung down to the floor. His feet trembled unceasingly. His toes had been cut off at the root. His body's position, his shortened torso seated on that contraption made him look like a ridiculous scarecrow, moving one to pity him more for this than for his wounds. Suddenly, the fisherman heard a voice coming through the pink bubbles that formed as the words made their awkward way through the hole that had once been his mouth.

"I wanted to speak to you, Peter. Just to you, because I know that though you are weak in spirit, your heart is bigger than your brothers' and fewer things distract you from your true destiny. You will follow me and upon my death, you will build the eternal word and with it you will make yourself invincible, and the powers of evil will not defeat you, nor will they defeat those who listen to you, those who will follow you. They have made me confess to terrible lies. The poor, those who have nothing to lose, they will know that these lies were the fruit of the pain, of the weakness of this wretched flesh. They will listen to you and with them you will be the founder of my family. You will be unable to shun your mission. Never again will your days be peaceful. Never again will you enjoy the happiness of your trade. Go now."

The old man was sobbing as he knelt before that talking body. With his handkerchief he tried to wipe clean that shapeless mass, that face, so removed now from the words it had uttered. An impatient movement shook the body making the tripod wobble:

"I told you already: leave me. Very soon I shall have to answer for the mission I was entrusted with here among men. Don't pity me. Pity yourself for the days that await you."

The old man got up and began walking back toward the door, never taking his eyes off the tormented figure. Just then, two men dressed in white and wearing surgical gloves came in carrying metal containers and jars.

"Leave us alone," they ordered. "We're going to fix him up so he can be displayed in public. There can be no trace of the guards' work. It's not an easy job and we've only a few hours left to do it. Come, get going, hurry up."

While one led him to the door, the other began arranging tweezers, knives and other instruments of various shapes and sizes on the table.

He was left alone in the corridor, not knowing where to go. He felt exhaustion making its way into his bones, pain piercing his insides, preventing him from thinking, from moving. He cried, he cried unceasingly as if a vessel somewhere, deep inside him, had broken and was now flooding out of control. Someone went by and gave him a shove, without seeing him. He heard the person excuse himself and answered back without hearing his own words. A long time went by. For him, these seemed like large, layered spaces of pain, of profound solidarity with people, vast, timeless spaces out of which he was rescued by the voice of one of the male nurses, who was handing him something no longer recognizable.

"Take this. He said it was for you to keep."

He reached out with his hand and felt the weight of a blood-soaked piece of cloth. He recognized the silk scarf and what had once been the stylized lines of racing sail boats but which now, with the effect of the dried blood resembled the confused traces of some ancient language printed on the fabric, as though they'd been worked over by humanity's ancient forgetfulness.

Like a sleepwalker he went into the courtyard and lay down against one of the lateral columns. Sleep overcame him. As he left wakefulness behind, a phrase came to him, one that he was to forget forever after, but which was the stuff of his nightmares that night: "Old, like fish whose marble flesh smells of hollyhock."

It was dark by the time he woke up. They had thrown an army blanket over him and he had wrapped it around himself in order to go on sleeping. He looked up at the stars and without understanding the depths of the night sky, fell asleep once again. The sounds of boots and weapons woke him up the next morning. He opened his eyes and saw a guard rinsing off his mouth and spitting a white liquid that smelled of mint into the courtyard drain. He felt numbness in his limbs from sleeping on the hard bed of tiles. A sergeant who had been watching him for a while came up to him and said:

"Hey, old man, you've slept off your drunkenness, now go. And don't get into trouble with the police again."

Peter looked at him and guessed by the colour of his insignias, that he belonged to a new regiment which had surely come to relieve the one from the previous day. They probably took him for one of those drunks who wander in a stupor after a night of noisy, sleepless inebriety, ending up in quiet respectable neighbourhoods. He got up with difficulty as a wave of dizziness and nausea passed before his eyes and settled in his mouth. The fresh morning air gave him enough strength to walk up to the exit door. He was beginning to believe that he had indeed ended up there due to some scandal in a tavern. As he was pushing the door open, a dry martial voice shouted:

"Hey! Where does he think he's going? Who told him he could go? Stop him!"

Someone grabbed him by the arm, making him turn abruptly. A corpulent half-dressed officer was eyeing him from head to toe, examining him with sleepy parsimony.

"The sergeant," answered Peter, "the sergeant said I could go, sir." And he pointed to the other end of the courtyard where the sergeant who had spoken to him was now cleaning his pistol.

"Sergeant," shouted the officer, "what about this one?"

"No, Captain. There's nothing against him. The shift from last night left no papers. It seems he ended up here drunk and was fined or something."

"Very well then. You can go now, but use your head next time."

The old man opened the door and entered a long dark corridor: the lights had already been turned off even though the morning light did not seep in yet. There, at the very end, sunlight the colour of apples spread its soft light without casting any shadows. The fisherman headed for the exit, still hesitant but more awake now, conscious that there was something waiting for him outside which would free him from the vague, uncomfortable load that weighed so heavily on his soul. Suddenly, when he was ready to cross the threshold, someone again called out to him from inside. It was the captain, who put his head out to ask him:

"Hey you! Aren't you one of the followers of the one they executed last night?"

"I don't know who he was, sir," was all he managed to answer. "I'm just one of the fishermen from down at the docks. My license is in good order. I've nothing to do with anyone who may have been executed. The license, you know, the waters around the base; but I've paid. I'm in the clear; I, you know…"

"That's fine," the captain interrupted cheerfully. "Get out of here and good luck to you." And the door was heard slamming leaving the hallway in darkness again.

As he crossed the doorway and felt the warm light in the street invade him, a cock crowed the four notes of his song to the sky, like an aerialist starting the show by throwing daggers into the air, before swallowing them. The bird's song inaugurated the morning, filling the air with the sounds man hears as he begins life anew on this earth.

The old fisherman went down to the docks. As he got closer

to the sea, familiar faces and places began to open the gates of the world for him. The days gone by began filling up with the unmistakable weight of memories, bitter and happy memories, the unchangeable substance of his life, prompting him once more to be a man among men, with no doctrines apart from the teachings of the ocean — its cunning, sudden fury and its unexpected, tiring calm. He got into his boat and began fine-tuning the engine. Contact with the tools, the purring of the motor, the sea air sweeping the soft wood off the deck, plunged him into his affairs, unburdening him of the oppressive weight that had been building up inside that deft pursuer of whales and tuna schools in the alienating presence of the Master. He got the motor going and set sail for the headquarters of the port authorities. He was going to renew his fishing license. The vibration of the propeller, the swirling water hitting the prow of the boat, completed his bond with the world, and he understood why he had denied the Master, how strange he felt his doctrine to be and what an impossible sacrifice it signified. Everything that had happened in the previous weeks began to recede, to find its proper place in the past, to find its place in his memory with other memories, losing that special energy, that vertiginous lure which had almost made him renounce his condition among men.

He washed the scarf in the water that rushed overboard and hung it to dry on one of the lateral portholes. The designs of those stylized yachts became visible again on the ivory and light blue silk background.

The Last Face

(A Fragment)

The last face is the face death dons to greet you.
From an anonymous manuscript in the Library
of Mount Athos, XIth Cent.

he pages you are about to read belong to a bundle of manu-
scripts sold at a book auction in London a few years after the
end of the Second World War. These writings had belonged
to the Nimbourg-Napierski family whose last surviving member
died at Mers-el Kebir, fighting as an officer for Free France. The
Nimbourg-Napierskis had arrived in London just months before
the fall of France bringing with them their most prized family
heirlooms: a saber with an ivory handle encrusted with rubies and
sapphires given by Marshal Joseph Poniatowski to Colonel of
Lancers Miecislaw Napierski as a memento of his heroic conduct
in the battle of Friedland; a series of sketches and drawings by
Delacroix purchased by Prince Nimbourg-Boulac from the artist;
the antique coin collection of the elder Napierski, who had died
in London a few days after they emigrated; and the aforemen-
tioned manuscript diaries of Colonel Napierski.

Colonel Napierski's papers ended up in my hands quite by
chance. As I leafed through them in search of details pertaining to
the battle of Bailén, which he discusses, my eyes stumbled over

two words and a date: Santa Marta, December 1830. I began to read, my interest in the defeat at Bailén quickly fading as I delved deeper and deeper into those tight lines written in the Colonel's round, clear handwriting. The folios were not in order so that I found it necessary to also search among eight volumes of dossiers which seemed to date from the same period, judging by the colour of the ink in which certain names and dates had been recorded.

Miecislaw Napierski had journeyed to Colombia to offer his services to the liberation armies. His wife, Countess Adehaume de Nimbourg-Boulac had died during the birth of her second son and the Colonel, an upright Pole, had travelled to the Americas in search of a place where freedom and sacrifice could breathe new life into his dreams of adventure, cut short by the fall of the Empire. He left his two sons in the care of his wife's family and set sail for Cartagena de Indias. When the frigate he was travelling on made port in Cuba, he was detained for some obscure reason and was then incarcerated in the fort of Santiago. He endured several years of imprisonment there until he managed to escape to Jamaica. In Kingston he boarded the frigate "Shannon" bound for Cartagena.

For reasons which will be seen later, we are transcribing only those pages which make reference to facts that deal with a man's death and the circumstances surrounding that death. We will omit all those commentaries by Napierski not relevant to this particular episode of Colombia's history because they tend to dilute and often blur the development and dramatic denouement of a life.

Napierski wrote this part of his diary in Spanish, a language he had good command of, having learned to speak it while in Spain during the occupation of the Napoleonic armies. The tone of certain paragraphs does betray the influence of the Polish poets exiled in Paris, who were his close friends — especially that of Adam Nickiewiez who had stayed at his house.

June 29. I met General Bolívar today. Such was my interest in catching his every word and noting his smallest gesture, and such are his powers of expression and the intensity of his thinking, that now, as I sit down to record on paper the details of our interview it feels as though I had known the Liberator for years, as though I had always served under his command.

The frigate anchored this morning in front of the fort of Pastelillo. An Aide-de-camp came to pick me up at around ten this morning. I went ashore with the captain, a British consular agent by the name of Page. When we landed we went to the "Foot of the Stern," a place thus called because it sits in the foothills of a mountain by that name. On the peak of the mountain is a fortress that once served as a convent for nuns. Bolívar moved there from the little town of Turbaco, thinking his stay would last but a few days.

We entered a large villa with cobblestone courtyards, full of half-wilted geraniums. Its thick walls give the whole place the look of an army barracks. We waited in a little room with uneven, rickety furniture and bare walls stained by the humidity. A little while later, Mr. Ibarra, Aide-de-camp to the Liberator, came in to say that his Excellency was just about finished getting dressed and would be joining us momentarily. Very soon after, a door I had assumed was closed, opened a sliver and a black man holding some clothes and a blanket in his hands, stuck his head out and signaled to Ibarra that we could now go in.

My first impression was one of surprise when I found myself in a large, empty room with coffered ceilings, a field bed against a corner and a night table stacked with books and papers. Here too, the walls were covered with water marks caused by humidity.

ÁLVARO MUTIS

There was a complete absence of furniture or decoration: a lonely faded chair with a high back, and the bottom coming out, faced a courtyard planted with orange trees in bloom, whose soft aroma blended with the overpowering smell of cologne from inside the room. For a moment I thought that we would be led to another room and that this was just the temporary bedroom of one of the assistants. Suddenly, a strangely hollow yet ringing voice denoting extreme physical weakness was heard from behind the chair speaking impeccable French, barely betrayed by a slight accent from the Midi.

"Come in, gentlemen, they're bringing us more chairs. Please excuse the scarcity of furniture but we are all just passing through here. I'm unable to get up to greet you. Please excuse me."

We went to greet the hero, while some soldiers, all with strong mulatto features, placed chairs in front of the one occupied by the sick man. While he spoke to the captain of the sailing ship, I had the opportunity of observing Bolívar. The lack of proportion between his slight body and his energetic, vivacious features feels odd. Especially the large dark and watery eyes which peek out from under the pronounced arch of his eyebrows. His skin is of an intense dark colour and yet through his thin batiste shirt one can glimpse a soft olive tone untouched by the ravages of the sun and the wind of the tropics. The prominent, magnificent forehead is furrowed by a multitude of fine wrinkles that appear and disappear constantly and give his face an expression of astonished bitterness, confirmed by the outline of his mouth bordered with deep lines. It reminds me of Caesar's face on that bust at the Vatican Museum. The pronounced chin and his fine, sharp nose lessen somewhat the overall impression of melancholic bitterness, suggesting instead a massive energy intensely focused on the person he is speaking to at the time. I was surprised by his long, slender, bony hands, their well-groomed, almond-shaped nails, so completely foreign to a life of battles and inhuman efforts lived out under the ravages of an implacable climate.

A gesture from the Liberator or *Libertador* — I had forgotten to mention that this was the title conferred by the Congress of Colombia on Bolívar and the one he is best known by, better even than his own name and his official titles — profoundly impressed me, as though it had been with him all his life. He touched his forehead very lightly with the palm of his hand, then slowly slid his hand down until he was able to hold his chin between his thumb and index finger. He remained like this for a long time, gazing fixedly at the person he was speaking to. I was engrossed in observing all his movements, when he suddenly asked me a question, thus interrupting a long explanation of the captain's about his European itinerary:

"Colonel Napierski, they tell me that you served under Marshal Poniatowski and that you fought with him in the defeat at Leipzig."

"Yes, your Excellency," I answered, angry at myself for having been taken off guard. "I had the honour of fighting under his command in the Lancers of the Guard and had to live through the terrible pain of witnessing his heroic death in the waters of the Elster. I was one of the few who managed to reach the other shore."

"I feel great admiration for Poland and her people," Bolívar answered. "They are the only true patriots left in Europe. What a pity that you have come so late. I would so have liked to have you as part of my staff." He remained silent for an instant with his eyes lost in the quiet foliage of the orange trees.

"I met Prince Poniatowski in the Paris salon of Countess Potocka. He was a charming, arrogant young man whose political ideas were somewhat vague. He felt a certain weakness for the manners and ways of the English, which he made too obvious, forgetting that Britain was the bitterest enemy of his country's freedom. I remember him as a man at once courageous to the point of recklessness and innocent to the point of folly. A dangerous mixture for the rugged roads to power. He died a great soldier. How many times on crossing a river (and I've crossed many in my life, Colonel), have I thought of him, of his enviable coolness under fire, his splendid daring. That's the right way to die, not this shameful, sorry pilgrimage through a country that neither loves me nor honours my service to it."

A young general with thick reddish sideburns respectfully interrupted the sick man with a voice broken by his own mixed emotions:

"A group of vile, bitter men is not all of Colombia, Excellency. You know how much love and gratitude we Colombians feel for you and all you have done for us."

"Yes," answered Bolívar with a rather surprised air. "You're probably right, Carreño, but none of the men you speak of were there when I left Bogotá, nor when we passed through Mariquita."

The meaning of his words escaped me, but I did notice a sudden look of shame, sensed an almost physical discomfort in those present.

Bolívar turned to address me with renewed interest:

"And now that you know that there's nothing left to do here, what are your plans, Colonel?"

"I will return to Europe," I answered, "as soon as possible. I must put family matters in order and try to save at least part of my patrimony, albeit small."

"We might be travelling together," he said to me, while also turning to the captain.

The captain began telling the sick man that they would now set sail for La Guaira and from there would come back to Santa Marta, and only then set sail for Europe. He indicated that he could accept new passengers only upon his return. This could take two to three months at most, because in La Guaira he was expecting a shipment coming from the interior of Venezuela. The captain stated that upon his return to Santa Marta he would be honoured to count the Liberator as a guest on the "Shannon" and would immediately proceed to make whatever arrangements were needed to furnish him with all the comforts required for his well-being.

The Liberator accepted the sailor's explanation with a kind, ironic gesture and commented:

"Alas, Captain, it almost seems written that I should die among those that cast me away. It would seem that I don't even deserve the consolation granted the blind Oedipus, who was able to turn his back on lands that so despised him."

He remained silent for a long time. All that could be heard was the labourious wheezing of his breathing and, now and then, the faint tinkling of a sword and the creaking of one of the old chairs we occupied. No one dared interrupt his deep meditation, evident to all those present thanks to his gaze, lost in the quiet air of the courtyard. His British Majesty's consular agent stood up finally. We all followed suit and went up to the patient to say goodbye. Unable to separate himself from his bitter and bottom-less thoughts, he looked at us as though we were mere shadows living in a world he felt completely absent from. As he shook my hand he nevertheless said to me:

"Colonel Napierski, feel free to come whenever you wish to keep this sick man company. We'll talk a bit about other times, about other lands. I think it will do us both good."

His words moved me. I answered:

"I will, Excellency. It is a pleasure and an honour to be able to visit you. The ship will be docked here for a few weeks. I will make good use of your invitation."

I suddenly felt stiff, my manner too ceremonious for that miserable room, especially after the straightforward tone the hero had used with me.

It is night time now. Not even a hint of wind. I go up to the deck of the frigate for fresh air. High above a flock of shrill birds, whose screams get lost in the stagnant, rancid waters of the bay, crosses the shadowy night. In the background lies the vigilant and angular outline of the fort of San Felipe. All this has a timeless feel to it, a strange atmosphere that reminds me of something encountered before, though I don't know when or where. Both the walls and the fort are like medieval reminders rising from the lianas and swamps of the tropics. The walls of Aleppo? The walls of Saint John of Acre? The Lebanese ruins perhaps? An admirable warrior's solitary struggle with death closing in on him in a ring of bitterness and disillusionment. When and where did I live this before?

June 30. Yesterday I sent one of the cabin boys to see how the Liberator was doing, whether I could visit him in case he was feeling better. He came back with news that the patient had spent a terrible night, that his fever had gone up. Bolívar wanted to personally let me know that he would inform me as soon as he was feeling better the next day, so I could visit him. As a matter of fact, General Montilla and an officer whose last name I didn't quite catch, came to get me today at two o'clock in the afternoon, the hottest time of the day. "The *Libertador* is feeling better and would delight in the pleasure of your company," explained Montilla, obviously repeating what the sick man had told him word for word. With Bolívar, the worldly man is always noticeable behind the military man, the politician. One of the charming things about his manner is that the brilliance so characteristic of men who frequent the salons of the Consulate, gives way to an almost homely military plainness that reminds me of Marshall McDonald, the Duque of Tarento and Count Fernán Núñez. Furthermore, there is the personal, local accent — a mixture at once fiery and whimsical which, and this is a well known fact, has made him very lucky with women.

They took me into the courtyard with the orange trees, where a hammock had been installed for him. Two nights of fever had left their mark on that face which now reminded me of a Phrygian mask. As I got up to greet him, he gestured me to take a seat in a chair they had just brought for me. He was unable to speak. Ibarra, the Aide-de-camp, whispered that he had just suffered a very violent coughing fit and had lost a great deal of blood again. I tried to remove myself so as not to inconvenience the sick man, but he raised his body ever so slightly and, in a husky voice that moved me because of all the suffering it betrayed, he said:

"No, no, please, Colonel, don't go. I will be fine in no time at all and we'll talk a little. It will do me much good. I beg you, please stay."

He closed his eyes. Vague shadows crossed his face. An expression of relief erased all the lines on his forehead, and softened those around his lips. He smiled, almost. I sat down as Ibarra withdrew in silence. When fifteen minutes had passed, he seemed to wake up from a long dream. He excused himself for having called for me, thinking he would be able to talk for a while. "Tell me a bit about yourself," he added, "what's your impression of all this?" He underlined the words with a movement of his hand. I replied that it was a bit difficult for me to formulate an exact opinion based on my impressions. I commented on the feeling I had felt while standing at night in front of the walled city of a vague and timeless immersion into something already lived out, I don't know where or when. He began to speak to me about the Americas, about the republics born of his sword which, deep down, he sometimes felt as foreign.

"All human undertaking is bound to be frustrated here," he commented. "The dizzying confusion of the landscape, the immense rivers, the chaotic weather, the jungle's vastness, the implacable climate, all these work against the will and undermine the deep, essential reasons for living we inherited from you Europeans. Those reasons still drive us on, but we tend get lost along the way with the rhetoric and the bloodletting violence that razes everything. Our consciousness of what we should have done and did not do remains with us and keeps working inside, turning us into an unhappy, conniving, frustrated, noisy and inconsistent lot. Those of us who left the best of our lives buried in these mountains, know only too well the extremes to which this sterile, twisted lack of conformity can lead. Did you know that when I demanded freedom for slaves, the clandestine voices that conspired against our project and prevented its fulfilment were those of my own comrades-in-arms? The very same people who had risked their lives crossing the Andes at my side to conquer the Vargas bog, Bocoya and Ayacucho. Yes, the same men who went to prison, who went through endless suffering in the jails of Cartagena, Callao and Cádiz at the hands of the Spanish. How can one explain this if not as stinginess, as feebleness of the soul, typical of men who are ignorant of who they are, who don't know where they come from, what their reason for being on this earth is? The fact that I've always known their true nature, that I've tried to modify and improve it, has now turned me into an uncomfortable prophet, a bothersome foreigner. This is why I am not wanted in Colombia, my dear Colonel. But a strange fate dictates that I should die when I am about to leave these lands, and this tells me that my place, my grave, is not over there, on the other side of the Atlantic."

He spoke with feverish passion. I tried suggesting that he rest, that he try to forget these things that can't be changed and are inherent to human nature. I brought to bear a few fairly obvious but painful examples in Europe's recent history. He remained deep in thought for a while. His breathing became regular and his eyes lost the delirious intensity that had made me fear a new emergency.

"It doesn't matter, Napierski, it's all the same; there's nothing left to do with all this," he commented, pointing to his chest, "we're not going to stop death's labour by keeping what we feel to ourselves. Better to let it out, less harm will come our way by speaking out to friends like you."

It was the first time he confided in me with such warmth, and this moved me, naturally. We went on talking. I mentioned the case of Europe again, the lack of direction in those that still longed for the glories of the Empire, the stupidity of leaders who were still trying to stop an irreversible process by means of cunning and the routine of committee work. I spoke to him about the Russian tyranny of my country, about our frustration, about the plans for an uprising we had prepared in Paris. He listened to me with interest, while a smile of scepticism etched itself across his face.

"You will overcome this crisis, Napierski; you've always overcome these periods of darkness. New times of prosperity and greatness will come to all of you, while here in America we will slowly sink into the chaos of civil wars, of sordid conspiracies. We will lose our energy in the process, we will lose our faith, all the things we need to make the most of this, the very reasons that can give meaning to the efforts that made us free in the first place. We are a hopeless case, Colonel. This is what we are, what we were born to be…"

The Aide-de-camp interrupted us. He was carrying an envelope which he handed over to the sick man, who recognized the handwriting immediately and explained to me with a smile:

"You will forgive my reading this letter right away, Napierski. It's from someone I owe my life to, someone who remains wholly faithful to me." I withdrew to a corner, let him be, while I talked about some of my plans to Ibarra.

When Bolívar had finished reading the two pages, written in small handwriting but with large capital letters that resembled arabesques, he called us to his side. He looked changed and, I should say, almost rejuvenated. We remained silent for a long time. He was contemplating the sky through the orange trees in bloom. He took a deep sigh and spoke to me in a light, almost flirtatious tone:

"This thing of dying young at heart has its advantages, Colonel. It is the one thing that not even miserly conspirators, not even the forgetting of those close to you, nor the whim of the elements can destroy — not even the decay of one's own body. I need to be alone for a while. Come by more often. You are one of ours, Colonel, and despite your magnificent Spanish, it's useful for us both to practice our French, lest it get rusty."

I said goodbye, glad to see him in better spirits.

Before going back to the frigate, Ibarra went with me to buy a few things in the city's downtown, which resembles that of Cádiz a bit, and that of Tunisia and Algeciras a great deal. While we walked along the white shady streets lined with houses full of balconies and roomy courtyards, their splendid vegetation inviting with their humid freshness, he told me about Bolívar's love affair with an Ecuadorian lady who had saved his life. With courage and serenity, she had alone confronted the conspirators who had gone to assassinate the hero inside the rooms of his San

Carlos palace in Bogotá. Many of the conspirators had been his comrades-in-arms. Almost all were men he himself had made. Now I understand the bitterness of his words earlier this afternoon.

July 1st. I have decided to stay in Colombia, at least until the frigate's return. Certain reasons, vague and difficult to jot down on paper, prompt me to stay next to a man who is heading straight to his death amidst the indifference, even the rancour, of those who owe him everything.

My original reason was to enlist in the army of Greater Colombia and, even though adverse circumstances have prevented my doing so, it is only natural that I should at least lend the simple service of my company and devotion to the man who organized those armies, leading them to victory through five nations. Though it is true that the five or six people who surround him show him boundless affection and loyalty, none of them can offer the comfort and relief our common education and memories provide. Despite the respectful distance of our relationship, I realize that there are certain subjects he discusses only with me and, in so doing, he feels as though he were bringing a friendship from his youth back to life. I notice this even when he speaks to me in French, in the turns of phrase that spring up, the type made fashionable in their salons by Barras, Talleyrand and Josephine's friends.

The Liberator has suffered a relapse from which he will not recover according to the doctor who looks after him, and of whose capabilities I grow more doubtful with each passing day. The cause was a piece of news he received yesterday. He was in his room lying on his field bed, taking a break from the chair on which he spends most of his time. Some brief but agitated whispering was heard and then, a knock at the door.

"Who is it?" asked the patient, sitting up.

"Mail from Bogotá, Excellency," answered Ibarra.

Bolívar tried to get up, but was forced to lie down again, shaking from a sudden fit of coughing. I handed him a glass of water. He took a few gulps and then asked his Aide-de-camp to come in. Ibarra was visibly upset, despite efforts at self-control. Bolívar stared at him and asked him intrigued:

"Who's bringing the mail?"

"It's Captain Arrázola, Excellency," he answered in a weak and mellow voice.

"Arrázola? You mean Santander's assistant? He is coming here to spy more than to bring news. Let's be done with it, let him in. But, what's wrong with you, Ibarra?" he asked the Aide-de-camp, seeing that he wasn't moving.

"My General, Excellency, prepare yourself for some terrible news."

The tears welling up in his eyes forced Ibarra to turn around and leave the room in a hurry. Outside he spoke to someone again. The sound of people running, grouping themselves around the man who had just arrived, could be heard. Bolívar remained motionless, his eyes fixed on the door. Ibarra came in again, followed by an officer in service uniform, whose faced was crossed by a thin, dark-coloured scar. His restless gaze wandered through the room until it came to rest on the bed from which he was being so fixedly watched. Standing at attention, he introduced himself.

"Captain Vicente Arrázola, Excellency."

"Sit down, Arrázola," said Bolívar, without taking his eyes off him. Arrázola remained standing, stiff as a rod. "What news do you bring from Bogotá? How are things there?"

"Very unsettled, Excellency, and I'm bringing news that will hurt you, I fear, and I feel guilty for having to be the one bearing it."

Bolívar's huge open eyes now stared into empty space.

"Few things could hurt me now, Arrázola. Settle down and tell me what this is all about."

The captain hesitated for a moment. He tried to speak, hesitated again and, taking a letter with the Colombian seal out of his briefcase, he handed it over to the Liberator. The latter ripped open the envelope and began to read the hastily written lines. At that very instant General Montilla tip-toed in, his eyes red, his face pale. A moan, like that of a wounded animal, came from the field bed, sending shivers down our backs. Bolívar jumped out of the bed like a cat and taking the officer by the lapels, screamed at him in a terrible voice:

"Bastards! Who were the wretched ones that did this? Who? Tell me Arrázola! That's an order!" He was shaking the officer with unusual force. "Who could have committed such a stupid crime?"

Ibarra and Montilla ran over to get him off Arrázola, who was now staring in horror and in pain. With one blow Bolívar had managed to wrench himself out of the arms that held him. He staggered over to the nearest chair and collapsed with his back to us. For a moment we were at a loss, until Montilla invited us to leave the room and allow the Liberator to be alone. As we left the room I seemed to notice that his shoulders were shaking up and down, driven by a secret, desolate sobbing.

I went into the courtyard. All those present seemed overcome by a deep sadness. I went up to General Laurencio Silva, with whom I have become friends and asked him what had happened. He informed me that the Grand Marshal of Ayacucho, Don Antonio José Sucre, had been assassinated in an ambush.

"He is the Liberator's most esteemed friend. He loved Bolívar as a father. His indifference to honours and his modesty had made him somewhat of a saint, or a child. For this we always respected him, and the troops adored him," he explained while he ran his hand down his face with a gesture of despair.

I remained at the "Foot of the Stern" all afternoon. I wandered through corridors and courtyards until, well into the night, I ran into General Montilla who, in Silva's and Captain Arrázola's company, had been looking for me to invite me to dinner.

"Don't leave us now, Colonel," Montilla begged me. "Help us by keeping the *Libertador* company because this news will do more harm to him than all his life's travails put together."

I accepted gladly and we sat at a table facing the fort of San Felipe. The conversation prolonged itself after dinner, without anyone daring to importune the sick man. Close to eleven o'clock, Ibarra went into Bolívar's room with a candlestick and a cup of tea. He remained there for some time and when he came out, informed us that the *Libertador* wished us to keep him company for a while. We found him lying on his bed, covered from head to toe in a sheet soaked in sweat from a fever which had risen alarmingly. His face had assumed the contorted expression of a funerary Hellenic mask: his eyes were wide open and sunken and seemed to disappear into their sockets so that by the light of the candles one had the distinct impression of staring into two large holes. When the sight of his fine, half-open lips was added to this, the impression was one of bitter emptiness without solace.

I went up to him and expressed my condolences for the death of the Grand Marshall. Without answering me, he held my hand in his for a moment. We sat around the bed not knowing what to say, what to do to distract the man from the pain that consumed him. In that deep, cavernous voice of his which seemed to fill the room with shadows, he asked Silva:

"How old was Sucre? Do you remember?"

"Thirty-five, Excellency. His birthday was in February."

"And his wife, is she in Colombia?"

"No, Excellency. She was waiting for him in Quito. He was

on his way to join her there."

Once again everyone remained silent. In an effort to bring down his fever, Ibarra brought in more tea and made him drink a few spoonfuls. Bolívar sat up in his bed. We placed some cushions to help prop him up and make him feel more comfortable. We started a conversation about nothing in particular, the kind people engage in just to avoid a specific topic, when all of a sudden, he began talking to himself for a bit, then addressed me directly.

"It's as though death were coming to me to announce its intentions with this terrible news. The scythe's initial blow to test the sharpness of the blade. How I wish you had met him, Napierski. The warmth of his slightly absent-minded eyes, the way he walked with his shoulders somewhat stooped and his body bent, gave one the impression that he was crossing a sitting-room trying to go by unnoticed. And that gesture of his as he touched the handle of his sword with his middle finger. His shrill voice, the way he lisped those elusive, whistled *ess's* which Manuelita used to imitate so well, to make him blush. His shy silences. His sometimes brusque, cutting answers, always clear and honest. Death must have surely taken him by surprise. He must have wondered, 'Why this crime?' as his last breath left him. 'You and I,' he once told me in Lima, 'we will die of old age, no one can kill us after everything we've been through…' Always a dreamer, always generous, always a believer, always willing to recognize the best virtues in people, virtues he cultivated in himself so effortlessly without even noticing. Berruecos… Berruecos… A dark pass in the Cordillera. A gloomy mountain and the monkeys' screams following him all day long. Bad people, those people… They always meant work for us. They never joined us openly. The most humiliated of all perhaps, those who benefited least from the Crown and were, therefore, most submissive, the weakest.

Worthless! All those years fighting, giving orders, suffering, governing, building — just to end up hounded down by the same, always the same, imbeciles. Astute politicians with a barber's soul, the notary's dirty tricks. They know how to kill while they go on flattering with a smile on their face. No one has understood a thing here. Death took the best ones. Everything is now left in the hands of the shrewdest, the most devious, those who will squander our legacy — won with so much pain, with so many deaths." He leaned back on the pillow. The fever made him shake slightly. He turned to Ibarra again.

"There will be no trip to France. We will stay, even though they don't want us here."

Retching with nausea, he collapsed on the bed. He vomited and almost lost consciousness with the sharp pain. A blood stain began to spread over the sheets, slowly dripping onto the floor. His gaze absent, he kept whispering deliriously: "Berruecos… Berruecos… Why him?… Why like this?"

Then he lost consciousness and fainted. Someone went to get the doctor. After a detailed examination he explained that the patient was at the end of his strength, that it was risky to predict the outcome of the illness, which he was unable to diagnose.

I stayed until early dawn at which point I went back to the frigate. I've meditated for a long time in my cabin and have just told the captain about my decision to stay in Cartagena, to wait here until he returns from Venezuela, which he estimates will be in two months. Tomorrow I will speak to my friend, General Silva, and ask him to help me find some lodgings in the city. The heat is rising, and the walls let off a smell of rotting fruit, of humid, salty carrion.

July 5. Mail from France came yesterday. I have news from my children and a credit note for my bankers' agents in Bogotá. My stay in Colombia becomes more bearable this way, and I am now able to remain as long as it is necessary. That is, until Bolívar's fate is decided.

I took a walk along the city walls in the company of Captain Arrázola this afternoon. We talked at length. I must admit I originally felt a slight ill disposition toward him because of the reticence on the part of Bolívar and those close to him, whenever his name was mentioned, but found in him not only a likable person, but an irreproachable soldier as well. That scar across his face is from the blow of a sword he sustained in the battle of Queseras del Medio, where he fought a whole battery until dusk almost single-handedly. He complains that his services have not been fully acknowledged, and the bitterness he harbours is not against anyone in particular. He blames instead the selfishness and negligence that reigns in the country. His dealings with politicians and those in the Congress of Bogotá, have taught him to cautiously hide his opinions. He admires Bolívar but believes him to be too idealistic. He makes the comparison with Santander, who — however colourless and devious — is efficient, good at scheming and plays up to the group of families who now begin to avidly reap the fruits of independence. The more I see of them, the more I get to know them, the more my impression of the people of this land is confirmed. They are supremely talented, graceful and easygoing in their manner, yet the ideas they harbour about the reality they live in are very unclear. They hold a hidden and somehow shameful nostalgia for the viceregal splendours which, through their lineage, their name and the extent of their possessions, should have brought them greater wealth than they got after independence. Or so they think. That is where Bolívar has an advantage over all of them. His youth, spent in splendid squandering in the Court of Madrid and the Parisian salons during both Consulate and Empire — his familiarity with people who maintained the best manners and caustic ideas of the *Ancien Régime*, all these have given him a different perspective and a clearer image of his destiny and that of the republics.

Arrázola told me a few things about last September's murder attempt. He pointed out that the pardon granted the guilty ones, the instigators of the crime, stems not so much from Bolívar's goodness, as from a particular trait in his character, a sceptical fatalism, a profound knowledge of what motivates people. Therein, I think, stems the detachment and distance that characterize his behaviour. Now I remember a phrase I heard him say a few days ago: "All contact with man sows the fatal seeds of disaster, bringing us closer to death." We spoke of his loves. His fancy for Manuelita Sáenz. But, behind it all — the same distance, the same detachment.

July 10. Today the Liberator told me a recurrent dream he's been having these last few days, which has him perplexed. We were discussing the importance that the Romans attached to dreams when he said:

"I'm going to tell you a dream that, save for a few changes, haunts me and whose meaning escapes me completely. I'd gone to sleep with my window open, and the aroma of the orange trees permeated my room. I was walking through the gardens of Aranjuez. I was feeling somewhat tired, as if my limbs ached from the long walk. The freshness of the landscape filled me with a sense of relief, bringing with it renewed energy. I suddenly felt that I had a long life before me. The gardens stretched out into the horizon in a soft winding manner. In reality, the only thing they had in common with the gardens of Aranjuez was the intense aroma of the orange trees and the light filtering through the bluish Castilian fog. I came to some stairs that led to a corridor: its leaf-covered roof blended into a shaded labyrinth and was crossed by quick, silent insects. I sat down on the first step of the stairs and as I reached in my pocket for a handkerchief to dry the sweat off my face, I realized that I was dressed in the style of the beginning of the century, with tight-fitting, cream-coloured pants and a navy frock, cut in the English style, with wide lapels and a raised collar. As I moved my hand toward my pocket watch to see what time it was, a cramp paralyzed it in the act. Born precisely where my watch was, this sharp pain rose to my chest making breathing difficult. I then figured out that by holding my breath and cautiously withdrawing my fingers from my pocket, I would succeed in fooling this torture, enabling me to take out my watch without the pain growing stronger. When I finally looked at the face of the watch, the pain had disappeared. As it turned out, the watch was made of a fragile substance, like paper, and when I took it out of my pocket, the hands had folded so that there was nothing to indicate the time. I felt suddenly ashamed and when I tried to hide the wrinkled object behind the ivy that crept up the pergola, I realized that someone was watching me from the top of the stairs. As a matter of fact, it was a woman of voluptuous shape and aggressive freshness, whose face remained hidden in the shadows of the trained vine. Her blouse, which was open down to her waist, left her large, firm breasts almost completely bare. And her skirt, which clung to her body with the breeze, revealed the double arches of her long, thick thighs which ended at the promontory of her sex. The woman spoke to me from the shadows: 'It's useless for you to hide your tracks, darling. They will grow back on your body when you least expect them, and that's when truth will harm you most.' 'Madam,' I answered with fear, 'I come with a letter of introduction given to me by my uncle. As far as I know, this part of the garden is open to the public and anyone can stroll here freely.' A cocky, warm and aggressive laugh shook the woman's body exposing one of her breasts, which also shook wildly as a result. A large, erect, dark nipple was left uncovered, resembling circles under some-one's eyes. 'It must be fear which makes you so refined,' she answered as she descended the steps, 'I just wanted to say that it's too late for you and me to tire ourselves with those hiding places by the river. You are practically nothing now, boy, despite those English suits and the French jewels you wear.' Her sad green eyes looked at me fixedly. The wings of her straight, salient nose tensed with agitated breathing, born of an unsatisfied desire for which I felt guilty, I know not why. By then, I too was beginning to feel excited. Yet something told me that if I tried to go up and touch the woman, the sharp pain would again return and para-lyze me. She passed next to me and said in her raspy voice: 'It's not worth it. Don't move. I'm not even going to say let's leave it for next time because I know that there will be no next time. Be brave, it's all you can do now, and you must do it properly.' I fol-lowed her with my eyes until she disappeared behind some shrubs crowned with irises. I suddenly felt abandoned and alone sur-rounded by the stifling disorder of the dark corridors I would have to go through in order to reach the exit. I was also afraid of the insects full of venom which came out of the leafy cover and lost themselves in the darkness, without so much as the sound of their buzzing to announce their presence. I entered the arbour. As I made my way, the vegetation became increasingly dense. The insects flew by me, excited by my presence. They were of a soft, feathery consistency, like little birds of inexhaustible vitality. The inside of the arbour was now a shining marble gallery. Leaning against the wall, a blind beggar was playing a guitar whose sound echoed in that fresh place as though it were a harpsichord. As I went by, the blind man spoke to me: 'For pity's sake, alms for the monument of Marshall Berruecos.' I began to confuse myself with the blind man and when the pitiless darkness of his gaze had already invaded me, a wrenching, ancient and familiar sadness woke me up abruptly."

The *Libertador* remained silent for a few minutes and raised his face as if questioning me anxiously. Something about him, a presence, a message, left an aroma of horror in my soul, a mournful warning I could not quite define. I tried to extricate myself from the situation with some superficial banality, but he interrupted me gently:

"Don't strain yourself, Napierski. You and I know what this means. I simply never imagined that it would present itself to me in this manner. The dream keeps changing, its message clearer at each turn. We'll see what it means."

An old familiarity with death makes itself evident to me in Bolívar, a man who, since his youth, must have been asking himself about his own end in the silence of his solitary orphan's soul.

Sharaya

Sharaya, the holy man of Jandripour, had been sitting by the gates of the city since time immemorial. Here he received his meagre alms from the townspeople as well as their increasingly rare prayers. A gray, crusty layer covered his body, his hair hung in greasy tangled shocks crawling with insects. Skin covered his bones forming impossibly dark angles which gave his motionless figure a stony, statuesque air. All this contributed greatly to the sorry state of abandon the people of that place had left him in. By now, somewhere in the foggy memories of their youth, only the old folk remembered the arrival of the slim monk. In those bygone days he had a certain air of worldliness about him as well as great eloquence in religious matters, one he would gradually lose as he conquered ever more vast, ever greater domains of knowledge through meditation, while sitting by the side of the road.

Despite the pitiful, almost non-existent attention he now got from the townspeople, and perhaps thanks to it, Sharaya was a most attentive observer of the life around him and knew, as few could, the intricate, selfish stories of the town as they wove themselves and then disappeared with the passing of time.

His eyes had acquired the sweet, fixed stare of domesticated animals, which some mistook for the tameness of the imbecile.

Others, undoubtedly wiser, recognized it as the sign of a complete, luminous perception of the deepest secrets of being.

Such was the Holy Man of Jandripour of the Lahore district.

The night immediately preceding his last day in this world had been rainy. The river rushed down the mountain swollen and roaring like a sickly beast, with untiring energy.

Thick drops slide down the skin of the parasol the women left behind at the time of the great drought. The rain is pounding down like a warning, like a signal prepared in another world. Never before has it sounded thus on the antelope's taut hide. Something tells me, something in me has understood the insistent message. An enormous puddle has formed where the water runs off the soft dome that is supposed to protect me. Everything will quickly dry up with the approaching heat. The warm, steamy air is beginning to rise and the snakes are going into hiding in their flooded nests. High above, a kite butts up and down awkwardly. It's yellow. A woman's song rises and purifies the morning like a shroud of forgetting. A man holds a thread and another one looks at me in protracted astonishment. He discovers me, and I enter his childhood, am a landmark, and am born into a new life. In his eyes: fear. Fear and compassion. He is unable to tell whether I am an animal or a man. He searches out my pain with a little piece of bamboo. He does not find it. He runs to the other man, who pulls him away without turning to look at me again. The Holy Man of Jandripour. It's been such a long time. Something now, many things: a monk. The vastness of my knowledge now reaches the horizon that curves without beginning or end. He comes back. He extends his hand until he touches me, this time without the cane he uses to protect himself. As distant as a star, as close as something I dream. It's all the same. His friend calls him over. The kite falls slowly as it searches out its own death. And it is born. The trees conceal it. It falls into the river. A long voyage awaits it until the paper fades. Only the skeleton will reach the sea; and it will sink to the bottom. Oysters and corals will build the solid shadow of what once was. Fish will lay eggs inside, while the crabs cover their young with sand. The eels may go there to die, and florescent fish will burrow in that soft, changing substance. There will be a little stir with the passing of the undertow and centuries later, a little eddy will surge up to the surface. Once this is done, everything will be as before. Time without borders like a voiceless scream in the white emptiness of nothingness. Prisoners of their illusory boundaries: they call this life. Morning announces itself with this truck. Two more. Several went by last night. Soldiers coming down from the mountains, nodding off after several nights without sleep, propped up by their rifles. The truck can't get through. It's stuck in the mud. The engine roars furiously, it stops, moans again. They cut some branches. More come. Tanks. Seven of them. They push it. It starts again. There's shouting. Miserable shouts born of their anger against the water, the mud. Now they sing. They sing the disaster, they sing their blood, their wives, their sons, they sing their scrawny cattle. Great Mother, Giver of Life. They die the obedient soldier's death, obedient to the grave. Peasants, weavers, blacksmiths, actors, the acolytes of the temples, the students, the educated, the thieves, the children of functionaries, the machinists, the rice men, men of the road. They all share the same name, the same face, the same death. Silence comes from afar like a great net from another world. The insects are waking up. That was a snake between the leaves. Perhaps the very one that crept up my leg last night: water and blood in cold, articulated scales. The mother of us all travels her domains and from her old fangs flows the lethal milk of millennia. The mourners would often come to ask me why they were grieving, while the smoke of the pyre carried off their dirty tents into the air. By then, words had long since proven completely useless to me and there was nothing I could have told them. They knew already anyway, albeit differently, blindly, uselessly, like blood finding its own course. They fear death, yet they will rest in it and will join its fecund task, and flowing down the river as ash, they will leave behind the bitter waft of a new life, food and nourishment for other worlds. It's gone, fled through the weeds. It can hear steps before anyone else can. Townspeople with carts. The bed for the newlyweds is a gift from missionaries. False, loud and rusty, the gold of their lovemaking. Then, they flee. The mayor and his dropsical wife. He lies when he comes to pray. The priests at the small temple. Uneven wheels that slip and sway on the worn gearbox. Incomplete lives, hardly the pieces of the great truth — more like that gray scab that soils the pool after bathing. Dirt slag, heart of wretchedness, stairs of waste. So sure of themselves in their urge to flee. Another, deeper destruction urges them on, the real, the single catastrophe in the crushing, restless darkness of their instincts. They turn to me again. The older ones. I don't know how to read their eyes. And it's too late now to tell them that it is impossible to escape what is everywhere. They are the ones who pray for faith to be granted them, the ones who work the land to feed the cattle that pulls the plough. And what a hindrance, those shabby belongings of theirs. They leave offerings for me: whatever they don't want to take with them, whatever is superfluous in their flight. The widow and her children. Circles under her eyes; sagging, dead breasts. Flowers from the temple. She doesn't dare throw them out, or leave them in front of the idols to be destroyed tomorrow by the same fury which gave them birth. She will not go far. She is marked, set apart, chosen among all the others. Andra, the one who danced naked in front of the Holy Man for an entire night. Her children will one day remember: "...she died on the way, as we fled Jandripour. Then, we raised her body on the top of the tallest tree and there she rested, visited by the winds, washed by the waters of the world. We watched over her for days on end, until she disappeared..." And yet, it will not be as they think. Not exactly. Other things will remain forever hidden from them, things they carry within themselves. The passing of their

Mother, Bearer of Death, the one who leaps like a jet of blood, the one who makes her bones thunder slightly, the one who is polishing the lymph in her spine. They turn around to look at their abandoned homes. Their desires and fears, their miseries and exaltations will follow them for a long time, like a shout trying to reach them as they make their way. Soldiers. The escort fleeing with the signal flags. I see him. He sees me. Letters and words. He looks at me. To go. He is not sure. The last one. Alone. Perhaps. I don't know where my loneliness comes from. He turns, he looks at me again and leaves after the others. A sword inventing the blue ribbon of its blade with the words of the war gods awkwardly etched on it.

When noon came, Sharaya stretched out his hand and took half an orange, not quite dried out yet, and began to chew at its tenaciously fragrant skin. The afternoon heat spread the fruit's aroma over a dance of crazed insects hitting the skin of the privileged one. The sound of the waters began to wane and the river went back to its original size. As the sun began to go down, a slight drowsiness began to take hold of the monk, filling him with the inexpressible beatitude of the dreamer, thereby uncovering the secret trails of his destiny.

Unsettled waters that leap and splash: the current's cold spray. Water from the mountains descending, dancing its way down in eddies, slowing down in the womb where it turns slowly, smooth, warm, protected by the hip's round chalice. The smell of spices as they burn them in the small marketplace and the sharp sound of instruments that tell the story they are dancing to. Laughter in the toothless mouth of the old beggar-woman, laughter of the flesh, that remembers and compares. The implacable link, the great sweetness of the flesh that weighs us down, hurting us; long afternoons with our blood rising and ebbing in surprising tides and the proximity of happiness, man's small happiness, sister of horror. A brief happiness, much like the happiness of the rat's teeth when it eats and chews. A vast ash pallium over the memory of the flesh. Voyage to the seat of our masters of yesterday. Shy shepherds, lords of a portion of the world who turn into punctilious merchants, patient, stubborn, dreamy and forlorn outside their island. The propellers bite the murky waters of the river mouth and the endless, yellowish stain announces the large, noisy city of functionaries where wisdom rises up the symmetrical stairs stained by the soggy soot of machines. Lands of reason. Men and women hurriedly crossing the square in the greasy mist of the evening sunset. Leaping colours, a glass fills up with lights that disappear and give way to blue and green: Drink, drink, drink, drink. The baptismal spray leaps, it leaps at the sombre passing of those unsatisfied, hard-working masters. Waters that run down our backs, baptized in the frayed shadows of the jungle, surrounded by shrieking birds and creaking insects. The skin of the wiser, older man wrinkles under his sagging nipples, drenched under the waters of truth, waters that wash away old and new concupiscence, the one that erases titles placed on vast stone constructions: mother of subtle arguments. Godfather and master, my second father measures the surface of the earth, the jackal is oblivious to the truth, bitter frog, father of the truth. And now, our final struggle with them, my brothers. Protests, mountain jails, the party and its clandestine ramifications working like the veins of a body that is waking up. I could have been master of this place at one time, things looked like they had peacefully settled into their natural order. I could have dictated the law right under my parasol. I could have moved them to good, to evil, depending on their destiny. I could have preached a doctrine and made them a little better. The commissioner, with his reddish mustache and sweaty nape, is at his headquarters, still arguing under the dirty lamp. That old, proven way of reasoning which they use to make their way, so sure of themselves yet so far from themselves, while their best, their surest powers drown: "Nobody knows why you speak to them. They are not interested and they don't understand why I am here: I don't either. You alone have all the answers, but they are useless to you. We will all end up in the same place. You are the monk. Not everyone can be a monk. They give their destructive anger, their fecund desires. Indifferent, you watch the black sun of your inner conquests. You are miserable and poor, like they are, but because the road you have travelled is so short it cannot count toward the long journey you set yourself, motivated as you are by the deceptive pride that binds you. Put yourself next to them, guide them, help me impose authority and deliver things in good order. They will then make do as best they can. You have lived, you have grown up with us, among us, you know that our reasoning is the only one made to man's measure. Everything else is madness. You know so." Pale cobra, skin of truth. I dream my return to a dream attached to the divinity that dares not utter the name to the father nor the mother of all the gods, fleeting ghosts, slaves of men. I dream my dream dreaming the dream of the man who lifts his foot into the elephant position, the one who says "do not fear" with the arch of his fingers; he is the bearer of the fire, he rides on the turtle's back. The hour is coming, it came hours ago, it comes endlessly.

Sharaya fell asleep and during that long, heavy afternoon in the abandoned town of Jandripour, the first units of the invading army began marching in. They set up their tents and lined up their vehicles. When the monk woke up, the village had been set on fire. The damp wood out of which the houses were made was crackling, bursting in the soft evening air, clouding the sky with tall columns of smoke. There were many of them. Trucks and tanks kept rolling in; the roaring noise they made indicated that it wasn't just a small advance party, but the brunt of the army. Someone, in one of those shrill, hard accents of the highlands, began giving instructions through a loudspeaker about the manner in which soldiers should protect themselves from those still trying to organize resistance. The rush lasted far into the night when a great silence fell upon the village and its surroundings.

They sleep, exhausted after the rush. They seriously believe in the redemption of nations, in equality, in putting an end to injustice, in the brotherhood of men. But, they themselves bring in a new chaos which also kills, they bring with them new injustice which will hail new misery. It is like the man who washes his hands in a stream of poisoned water. Here come two. They light the way, lanterns in hand. They are peasants too. And they are young, children almost. There's a woman with them. Perhaps she is a prisoner, perhaps a whore following them for something to eat, for a little money. They tear off her clothes. That old, repeated rite, without faith and without love. Their hands and knees shake. Ancient shame upon the world. She laughs, her skin answers back and her limbs respond to the wave that grows in her body and presses her against the ground. Necessary mother. They are born again, united in the place of our beginning. They moan and laugh at the same time. One body with two drunken heads, heads wounded in the vertigo of their own rebirth, their long agony. The other one smiles timidly. He smiles at his own shame and waits. The children are sown on the liberated earth. They are gone. She gets dressed. The other one points the light of the lantern at me.

The soldiers and the woman stood there, engrossed in that strange jumble of dirty rags, rotten food and mummified flesh: the monk. They avoided Sharaya's fixed, burning eyes, witness of the brief pleasure they had stolen from their dark, transitory life. Very little of what one could call human flesh remained of the holy man. The woman was the first one to move her eyes away from that hieratic figure. She began covering herself with her clothes. The two soldiers, still intrigued, went up closer. Finally, the one who had been waiting by the side reacted abruptly: "He looks like a monk," he said, "but we can't let him watch as our troops march on. He's seen us already and has undoubtedly counted the number of trucks and tanks we have. Besides, nobody will now come to consult or worship him. His knowledge is finished." The other one shrugged his shoulders and without turning around, took the woman by the arm and went off down the white tracks that spotted the road. Before catching up to them, the one who had spoken raised his machine gun. With indifference he aimed at that wizened figure and pulled the trigger on the absent eyes, fixed on the perpetual disaster of time.

My passing was foreseen in each one of those quivering leaves. This very scene is so familiar to me, as to seem completely foreign. When the little owl finishes circling the high nocturnal sky, the meagre wish of those powers that bind us, will be done... the one who kills me... I, now reborn at the threshold of the world, perishing briefly like a flower that falls, like the uncontrollable saline tides leaving behind the bitter taste of life in our mouths: dying, running down the indifferent ground of the wretched dead star, traveller of that circular, empty nothingness, burning impassively, forever, forever, forever.

The Strategist's Death

A few facts surrounding the life and death of Alar the Illyrian, Strategist of Empress Irene for the Thema of Lycandos, came to the attention of the Church at the Council of Nicaea when it discussed the canonization of a group of Christians who had been martyred at the hands of the Turks in an ambush in the sands of Syria. In the beginning, Alar's name had come up together with that of the other martyrs. The one who eventually set the record straight was Nicephorus Callistus, Patriarch of Laconia, after he carefully examined some of the documents pertaining to the Strategist and his family, documents that shed new light on the life of Alar and dismissed any possibility of his being enthroned on the altars of the Church. When the letters of Alar to his brother Andronicus were finally made known to the Council, the Church imposed a dense silence around the Illyrian, and his name went back to the obscurity whence the ambitions of the Eastern Church had briefly rescued it.

Alar, called "the Illyrian" because of his inset, almond-shaped eyes, was the son of a high-ranking official of the Empire who had enjoyed the favour of the Basileus at the time of the struggle against the images. The skillful courtier had not occupied himself too greatly with his son's upbringing and arranged for him to be educated in Greece under the tutelage of the last Neoplatonists. In the confusion that reigned in decadent Athens, Alar lost all vestiges of his faith in Christ, if ever he had had any. Not that his father had distinguished himself for being pious. His high position in the court was more the fruit of an inexhaustible reserve of diplomatic subtleties than religious fervour. When the young man returned from Athens, however, his father could not help but express his surprise at the careless, rash manner in which his son referred to matters concerning the Church. The Empire was going through the cruelest period of iconoclast persecution, and the Mangana Palace was rife with mortal theological and liturgical traps. People better placed than Alar, more influential with the Autocrat, had lost their eyes, and even their lives, for some careless phrase or small sign of impoliteness at the Temple.

By means of skillful excuses, Alar's father arranged for the Illyrian to join the Emperor's army: the young man was named Turmarch of a regiment with headquarters at the port of Pelagus. It was there that the career of the future Strategist began. For a man of arms, Alar did not possess very solid virtues. A certain scepticism about the vanity surrounding military victories and no interest whatever in the grave consequences of defeat made him a mediocre soldier. Yet few could equal the humanity of his manner, the hearty popularity he enjoyed with his troops. In the worst of the battle, when everything seemed lost, men would turn to look at the Illyrian, who kept a cool head and always fought with a bitter smile on his lips. This was sufficient for them to get their courage back and come out victorious.

Alar had learned the Syrian, Armenian and Arab dialects with great ease and could speak Latin and Greek fluently. His accounts of the campaigns had earned him a certain renown among high-ranking officers because of the clarity and elegance of his writing style. By the time Constantine IV died, Alar had risen to the rank of General of the Army Corps and was commander of a garrison in Cyprus. Far away from the dangerous intrigues of the court, his military career allowed him to remain on the sidelines of the religious struggles which had brought such bloody repression to the Eastern Empire.

During a trip that the Basileus Leo made to Paphos in the company of his wife, the beautiful Irene, the young couple was received by Alar who successfully won the warmth of the new autocrats, especially that of Irene, the clever Athenian. She was flattered by the General's sincere enthusiasm and sharp erudition concerning Hellenic matters. For his part, Leo found special pleasure in his relations with Alar and felt a certain attraction for the Illyrian's straightforward, frank manner, as well as the irony with which he dealt with hazardous political and religious topics.

Alar had by then reached the age of thirty. He was tall, with a tendency to softness. He was slow in his movements and expressed his feelings cautiously through his ironic, half-closed eyes. He never lost his cordiality, which was military and direct in style. He could remain absorbed for days on end, reading, preferably the Latin poets. Virgil, Horace and Catullus were his companions wherever he went. He took great care in his attire, but wore his uniform only on special occasions. His father had died at the height of his political prestige, a prestige later inherited by Andronicus, the Strategist's younger brother, for whom Alar felt great affection and with whom he shared a deep-seated friendship. Before he died, the old courtier had asked Alar to marry a young woman from the upper Byzantine bourgeoisie, the daughter of an old friend of the family. Alar honoured his father's wishes and took her as his wife, yet he always found an excuse for living away from home without completely breaking the mandates and traditions of the Church. He was not known for the affairs and scandals that were common in those days among the high officials of the Empire. This was not due to coldness or indifference, but to a natural tendency to reflection and daydreaming, no doubt born from an early scepticism about people's passions and concerns. He enjoyed visiting the ruins that bore witness to men's vain attempts at the perpetuation of their deeds. Hence his preference for Athens, his liking for Cyprus and the risky incursions he made into the sleepy sands of Heliopolis and Thebes.

One time, when the Augustus named him Hypatos and entrusted him with the mission of arranging the marriage of the young Basileus Constantine to a Sicilian princess, the General stayed in Syracuse longer than was required. Then, he disappeared into the Tauromenium, where his officers had to go and seek him out in order to convey the peremptory orders of the Despoena, who was summoning him to appear before her without delay. The Basilissa had completely lost her patience by the time he appeared in the Room of the Dolphins. His voyage had dragged out longer than was reasonable due to his visits to the small ports and coves that line the African coast, where hidden Roman and Phoenician ruins were still to be found.

"You use the Caesar's time in a manner deserving of the severest punishment," she scolded him. "What explanation can you give for your delay? Perhaps you forget why we sent you to Sicily? Are you not aware that you are a Hypatos for the Autocrat? Who said you could enjoy your leisure time and dispose of it while serving the Isapostol, the Son of Christ? Answer me! Don't just stand there. This is the wrong time for such things, and I am not in the mood for your strange excuses."

"Madam, Daughter of the Apostles, Blessed One of Theotokus, Light of the Gospels," answered Alar unperturbed, "I made stops in search of traces of the divine Ulysses, inquiring about the veracity of his cleverness. It was not wasted time for the Empire. Neither was this time spent against the holy will of your plans. It did not seem fitting that someone of your son's rank, the Porphyrogenitus, should marry someone who is so obviously not his equal. Furthermore, it did not seem appropriate that I send you my reasons for not wanting to negotiate with the Sicilian princes, either by messenger or in writing. Their daughter is secretly engaged to one of the heirs of the house of Aragon. They made public their interest in a marriage with your son for the sole purpose of giving more weight to the conditions of the contract. As soon as they saw my obvious lack of interest in dealing with this matter, they themselves realized the uselessness of their plan. As far as my trip back is concerned, alas, Chosen One of Christ, it is entirely true that I was waylaid by desires weaker than my will to come before you."

Though Irene was not entirely convinced by the Illyrian's specious explanations, her anger had almost completely disappeared. As a warning that he not fall into error again, Alar was assigned to Bulgaria with the mission of recruiting mercenaries.

In the dusty garrison of a country particularly unpleasant to him, Alar underwent the first of the many changes to his personality that would follow. He became somewhat taciturn and lost the permanent good humour that had earned him so many close friends among his comrades in arms at court. Not that he seemed irritated, or lost his virtue for treating each and every one with the gentle familiarity of someone who knows well the ways of people. Yet, he often appeared distracted, his gaze fixed on empty space, as if expecting it to provide him with answers to the anguish that so perturbed his soul. His dress became simpler, his life more austere.

In the beginning, this change was perceived only by those closest to him and, both in the army and at court, he continued to enjoy the favour of those who professed friendship and admiration for him. In a letter that the Oikoumene Andreas, a close friend of Alar's and an expert in Oriental religions, wrote to Andronicus informing him of his interview with the latter's brother, the venerable one recounts the Illyrian's words and deeds. These were to contribute significantly to dashing the canonization project. He says, among other things:

"I met the General in Zarosgrad. When I arrived, he was recruiting mercenaries and was occupied with their training. I could find him neither in the city, nor in the barracks. He had had his tent set up on the outskirts of town, by the edge of a stream, in the middle of a grove of blooming orange trees whose aroma he is partial to. Even though he welcomed me in his usual cordial manner, I found him distracted, somewhat absent. There was something in his gaze that made me feel vaguely guilty and insecure. He observed me in silence for a while and suddenly, just when I expected him to inquire about you, about life at the court, about his people back home, he turned to me and asked: 'Which is the god that draws you to the temple, venerable one? Which of them all?' 'I don't understand your question,' I answered. And, without ever referring to the matter again, he began putting forth, one after another, all manner of strange details on the subject of the Persian religion and the Brahmins' sect. I thought him feverish at first. It was then that I understood that he was suffering a great deal, that these doubts hounded him like fierce dogs. As I was outlining some of the steps leading to Hindu perfection, or nirvana, he jumped up and shouted: 'No, that's not the way either! It is useless. There is nothing we can do. There is no sense in doing anything. We are trapped.' He lay down on a old contraption made from animal furs which serves as his bed and covered his face with his hands. He once again became immersed in thought. After a while, he apologized by saying: 'Forgive me, venerable Andreas, but having spent two whole months swallowing the red dust of Dacia, listening to the shrill language of these barbarians, I find it difficult to control myself. Pardon me and go on with your explanation. It is very important to me.' I continued my exposition, but I had lost interest in the subject, worried as I was by your brother's earlier reaction. I began to understand how deep the crisis he was undergoing truly was. As his brother and closest friend, you know full well that the General complies with his religious duties only as a formality, as part of the discipline and example he owes his troops. His complete separation from our Church and other religious beliefs is no mystery to anyone. Because I am keenly aware of his intelligence and have discussed this with him on so many occasions, I have no intention of con-verting him. However, I do worry, given that the Reverend Metropolitan Michael Lakadianus exercises so much influence over our beloved Irene, and has always shown so little sympathy toward your family. I fear that he might find out the details about the Illyrian's situation and bring harm to him by mentioning the matter to the Basilissa. I am telling you this so that you can pro-ceed on behalf of your brother and keep alive the affection he has always enjoyed. Before I move on to other matters not pertaining to the General, I want to tell you how our meeting ended. We both got sidetracked discussing the rituals that certain heretical Christian groups share with Eastern religions. By the time he had gotten over his initial fears and our conversation had drifted to the mysteries of Eleusis, the General began to speak more to him-self than to me, giving free rein to his interest in the Hellenes. You are well aware of his inexhaustible erudition on the subject. He suddenly interrupted himself and, looking at me as though he had just woken up from a dream, all the while caressing the funerary mask you sent him from Crete, he said: 'They alone found the way. By creating gods in their own image and likeness they gave transcendence to that eternal, ever-present inner har-mony from which truth and beauty flow. They believed in this harmony above all things, adored it and sacrificed everything to it. This is what makes them immortal. The Hellenes will outlive all races, all peoples, because they modelled on human beings those powers that can defeat nothingness. It is not a small thing, and it would be an impossible achievement now that the dark seeds of destruction have penetrated us so deeply. Christ sacrificed us on his cross, Buddha sacrificed us in his renunciation, Mohammed in his fury. We have begun to die. I do not explain myself clearly enough. And yet, I believe that we are doomed, that we have done ourselves the irreparable damage of falling prey to nothingness. We are nothing already, we can do no more. No one can act any longer.'

"He embraced me affectionately. He said no more. He opened a book and began to read. As I was leaving, I had the certainty that our dearest friend, your beloved brother, had set out on the road to a negation without limits, with implacable consequences."

The Oikoumene's worries were understandable. In the court political passions could become dangerously confused with the doctrines of the Church. Irene was increasingly falling prey to the religious intransigence that would prompt her to order the gouging of the eyes of her own son, Constantine, because she suspected him of sympathizing with the iconoclasts. Had Alar's words been merely uttered in court, his death would be certain. That is why, even though these matters were his chief preoccupation, the Illyrian was extremely careful not to discuss them with anyone, not even his closest friends. Once the period of oblivion in Bulgaria came to an end, his brother, who was deft at avoiding all dangers, obtained Alar's promotion to the highest of all military positions in the Empire: the rank of Strategist, personal delegate and direct representative of the Emperor for the Themas of the Empire. His appointment was not contested by any of the factions vying for power. Both sides were certain that neither could rely on the Illyrian to advance their political ends, and both parties consoled themselves with the thought that neither adversary would be able to count on the Strategist's favour. Furthermore, all of the Basileos were well aware of the Illyrian's lack of interest and detachment from anything related to political power or personal ambition, and knew that the Empire's forces would thus remain in loyal hands, never to be turned against them.

Alar travelled to Constantinople to receive his investiture from the hands of the Emperors. The Autocrat decorated him with the symbols of his new rank, and the Despoena handed him the eagle of the Stratoiti, thrice blessed by the Patriarch Michael. As Alar was taking the oath of obedience, the Emperor's eyes filled with tears. Years later, many cited this detail as a premonition of Alar's sad end and Leo's tragic demise. The truth was that the Emperor had been moved by the austere, almost monastic manner in which his friend of so many years had accepted the highest symbol of trust, the largest delegation of power a citizen could receive, after that of the imperial purpura.

A great banquet was held at the Hiera Palace. The Strategist did not mention or thank the Augustus for the immense honour conferred upon him. Instead, he engaged Leo in a long, exceedingly cordial dialogue concerning texts discovered by monks on the island of Prinkipo and which could be attributed to Lucretius. Irene interrupted their animated conversation more than once, at one point imposing a fearful silence upon all those present. "I fear," pointed out the Despoena, "that our Strategist was thinking more of the texts of the pagan Lucretius, than of the holy sacrifice made by our Patriarch on behalf of his soul's salvation." The Strategist's answer was memorable. "Truth to tell, Augusta," answered Alar, "that during the Holy Mass I was greatly preoccupied by the text attributed to Lucretius, but precisely because of the similarities that some of the passages bear to our own Scriptures, the only difference being that the Word that renders eternal the truth of the Scriptures is absent from the Latin. Furthermore, the text could be easily attributed to the prophet Daniel, or the letters of Paul, the Apostle." Alar's answer put everyone at ease and disarmed Irene who had posed the question largely at the urging of the Metropolitan Michael. But the Strategist understood that his friend had fallen irreparably prey to the blind fanaticism that would prompt her to shed so much blood, starting with her own household.

And here ends what could be said to be the public life of Alar the Illyrian. It was his last time in Byzantium. He was to remain until his death in the Theme of Lykandos, on the border with Syria, and it is there that all vestiges of his active, efficient administration are to be found. Alar erected numerous fortresses, military barriers against the Muslim invasions. He regularly visited every one of the border posts, no matter how wretchedly poor or how forsaken in the arid rocks and the burning sands of the desert.

He led a simple soldier's life assisted by those he trusted most: some Macedonian knights, an elderly rhetorician for whom he felt particular affection, even though he wasn't greatly gifted or exceptionally cultivated, a Provençal minstrel who had joined Alar during his visit to Sicily, and his personal guard of Khazars, recruited by him in Bulgaria, who answered only to his orders. His elegant attire gradually gave way to simple military dress to which he added the blessed eagle of the Stratioti on review days. Always by his side in his military tent were certain books — Horace, infallibly — the Cretan funerary mask given him by his brother, and a small statue of Hermes Trismegistus, a souvenir from a Maltese woman friend, owner of a pleasure-house in Cyprus. His closest friends became accustomed to his long silences, his strange distractions and the severe melancholy that showed on his countenance at sundown.

It was evident that the Illyrian's lifestyle greatly contrasted with that of the other Strategists of the Empire, who lived in sumptuous palaces and had people address them as "Sword of the Apostles," "Guardian of the Divine Theodahad," or "Favourite of Christ." They made an ostentatious display of their power and lived in scandalous squandering and luxury, sharing the Emperor that hieratic distance, an arrogant pomposity meant to awaken in their subjects a veneration and respect one could easily mistake for religious submissiveness. The case of Alar the Illyrian was unique, and his example was later followed by the wise Emperors of the Comneni dynasty with good political results. Alar lived with his soldiers. Escorted only by his Khazars and a regiment of Macedonian knights, he travelled constantly to inspect the frontier posts of his Theme, which bordered the domains of the tireless and avid Ahmid Kabil, a little Syrian king who sustained himself through ill-gotten booty from his incursions into the villages of the Empire. Kabil sometimes allied himself with the Turks against Byzantium, but they would occasionally abandon him in order to sign peace treaties with the Autocrat in neutral complicity.

The Strategist was known to suddenly appear at fortified posts, and remain there for weeks on end, supervising the progress of the construction work, as well as observing the morale of his troops. Like the rest of the men, he would put up in the barracks, where a narrow, whitewashed room had been set aside for him. Argiros, his orderly, would lay out a bed made of the animal furs he had grown accustomed to during his Bulgarian mission. While in residence, Alar administered justice, held discussions with architects and builders and audited the accounts of the chiefs of that particular stronghold. Then he would leave just as he had arrived, without disclosing where he was heading next. Vestiges of his affection for ruins and his interest in the fine arts, were still evident. They would come to light when decorations for a bridge or embellishments for a facade had to be chosen — when such matters as the recapturing of treasures from Ancient Greece, which had fallen into Muslim hands, came up. More than once he had chosen to rescue the torso of a mutilated Venus, or a Medusa head, over the relics of one of the Patriarch Saints of the Eastern Church. He was not known for carrying on love affairs or scandalous adventures, and he never showed any inclination toward the noisy orgies that other Strategists revelled in. At the beginning of his mandate he brought with him a young slave girl from Wales who served him with quiet tenderness and discreet devotion. But the young woman was killed when part of his escort fell into an ambush. From then on, he contented himself with spending the odd night at a sea port in the company of tavern girls with whom he could joke and laugh as he would with any of his soldiers. There was always that solitary, inner distance about him which awakened a certain undefined fear in young women.

Along with the gray routine of military life, the former glory of the Illyrian began to fade, and his life slowly began to fill with shadows — shadows he rarely alluded to and which never became the subject of conversation among those closest to him, simply because he would not allow it. The court forgot about him, or very nearly so. The Basileus died under strange circumstances. A few weeks later Irene proclaimed herself "Great Basileus and Autocrat of the Romans" in Saint Sophia. The Empire succumbed once again to one of its habitual periods of blind fanaticism and rabid theological hysteria. The all-powerful monks imposed the dark horror of their intrigues and led their victims either to the basements of the Blachernae, where their eyes were gouged out, or the hippodrome where they were dismembered by

spirited horses. This is how the slightest tepidity in someone's service to Christ and his Divine Daughter, the Morning Star, the
Divine Irene, was paid for. Yet no one dared to raise his hand
against the Strategist. His prestige in the army was solid. His
brother had been named Protosebastus and Great Master of the
Schools. Besides, the Augusta was well aware of the Illyrian's
aversion to taking sides, as well as his scepticism about the sav-
iours of the Empire, who kept appearing from nowhere.

It was around this time that Ana the Cretan appeared and
Alar's life changed completely once again. She was the young
heiress of the Alesis, a rich family of merchants from Sardegna
who had long since established themselves in Constantinople.
They enjoyed the confidence and favour of the Empress, whom
they often helped with sizeable loans. These were, in turn,
strengthened by revenue from taxes they collected from
Byzantine ports in the Mediterranean. Together with her older
brother, the girl had fallen into the hands of Berber pirates as they
made their way back to Constantinople from Sardegna, where the
family owned several large properties. Irene had entrusted the
Illyrian with the recovery of the Alesis, which he would have to
negotiate with the Emir's delegates. As protector of the pirates,
the Emir collected interest on their plunder.

Before recounting the encounter with Ana, however, let's
look into the Strategist's thoughts, his certainties and doubts, at
the time of his meeting the woman who would bring such deep,
new-found happiness to his last days, and would give his death its
particular purpose and meaning. There exists a letter from Alar to
his brother Andronicus written four days before he greeted the
caravan of the Alesis. After commenting briefly on the news
about the Empire which his brother had earlier conveyed to him,
the Illyrian goes on to say:

"...this only reinforces my conviction that politics means a dangerous compromise of man's best virtues. Just observe the rationalizations our Basilissa must now use to impose order in Byzantium, measures which she herself would have rejected ten years ago as constituting not only an attack on the laws of the Empire, but a heresy. Look how many people have perished in the past for harbouring the very ideas she pursues today. So many people blinded, maimed for having publicly practiced a faith which now stands as the official faith of the State. In his mind's miserable confusion, man builds complicated architectures thinking that if only they were rigorously applied, he would succeed in bringing some order to the tumultuous, chaotic beating in his blood. Our hands are caught in a trap of our own making, and there is nothing we can do. And no one expects us to do anything. Any decision we make is bound to get lost like those torrents of fresh water which flow from faraway places into the sewage drains, only to become confused with the vast expanse of the ocean. You may think that a bitter scepticism prevents me from enjoying a world freely bestowed upon us. Such is not the case, dearest brother. A great tranquillity visits me, and each episode of my routine as governor and soldier comes to me in a new light, revealing to me unsuspected sources of life. I don't look into each and every thing for improbable, obscure meanings. I try instead to rescue from life a presence that will reveal to me the reason for each day. I know, with complete certainty, that any communication one may attempt with one's fellow man is in vain, useless. I also know that only through the dark roads of the soul, only through the ever-present harmony which outlives all civilizations and empires, will we be able to save ourselves from nothingness. I am thus able to live without fooling myself and without expecting others to do so for me. My soldiers obey me because they know that I have more experience than they have in this daily dealing with death which is war. My subjects accept my failings because they understand that they are born not of written laws, but of what my natural love for them tries to understand. I have no ambitions whatsoever; a few books, the company of the Macedonians, Dario's subtleties, the song of Alcen the Provençal and the warm bed of a Lebanese Hetaera, fulfil all my hopes and aspirations. I am not in the way of anyone, and no one stands in my way. In battle, I kill without mercy, but without fury. I kill because I wish our Empire to last as long as possible, before the barbarians flood it with their harsh jargon and their angry prophet. I am Greek, Eastern Roman, call it what you will, but I know that the barbarians, be they Latin, German or Arab, be they from Kiev, Lutecia, Baghdad or Rome, will end up erasing our name and our people. We are the last heirs to immortal Hellas, the only ones capable of giving man a valid answer to his most fundamental questions. I believe and know, in my capacity as Strategist, one which I carry out fully, that what one can do is limited. I also know that doing otherwise would be worse than death itself. We lost our way centuries ago and have given ourselves over to a bloodthirsty Christ, whose sacrifice weighs down man's heart with injustice, making him distrustful and unhappy, making him a liar. We have walled up all the exits and continue to fool ourselves, as animals in the darkness of their circus cages are fooled into believing that the jungle they painfully miss is outside, waiting for them. What you tell me about the ambassador of the Holy Roman Empire is a good example of what I think. As Logothete of the Empire, you should try to make him see how dismal his intentions are, how wrong his ideas. And yet, this would be like…"

It was dusk by the time the Alesis' caravan reached the fortified post of Al Makhir, where the Strategist had set up camp to wait for the arrival of the hostages. The Illyrian had retired early. He had done three days of travel without sleeping. The next morning, after giving orders to dismiss the Turkish cavalry which had brought them there, he gave audience to the rescued citizens of Byzantium. They entered the Strategist's small cell in silence and could barely believe their eyes when they saw the Protosebastus of Lycandos, the Armed Hand of Christ, Beloved Son of the Augusta, living like a simple officer, without carpets or jewels, just a few books to keep him company. He was lying on his bed made of bear skins and was going over some accounts, when the Alesis came in. They were five, headed by a serious, self-absorbed looking young man, and a woman, who was about twenty years old and wore a veil over her face. The remaining three were the family doctor, an administrator from their house in Bari and an uncle who was an Oikoumene of the Studion. They paid the Strategist the tributes due someone of his rank. When they were done, he invited them to sit down. He read out the names of the visitors and each one answered in the usual manner: "Greek by the grace of Christ and his redemptory blood, Servant of the Divine Augusta." The girl was the last one to answer. As she spoke she lifted the veil off her face. Alar did not notice her at first, but the calm seriousness of her voice, not typical of someone her age, caught his attention.

He asked them a few questions, out of courtesy, inquired about their trip and spoke at length to the Oikoumene about his friend Andreas, whom the latter knew superficially. The young woman answered Alar's questions with details that pointed to a clear intelligence and a sharp sense of discernment. The Strategist became engrossed in the conversation and the audience went on for several hours. Taking up the thread of an observation of her brother's about the splendours of the Emir's court, the girl asked the Strategist: "Because you have renounced the luxuries that your position presupposes, and since you lead a seemingly monastic life, we must assume that you are a man of profound piety." Alar stared at her. He forgot the words she had used to pose the question, but grew increasingly more surprised by a secret harmony, which felt ancient and which revealed itself in the young woman's face. Just as with the Cretan mask, this harmony mixed itself with a seemingly otherworldly well-being, conferred to it by that age-old interrelation of eyes and mouth, nose and brow — a fullness of shape characteristic of some nations of the East. The young woman's smile brought him back to the present. This is how he answered: "This type of life agrees more with my personality than with my religious convictions. I regret not being able to offer you better lodgings."

This is how Alar met Ana Alesi, the one he would later refer to as "the Cretan," the one he would love until his final days and who stayed by his side during his last years as Governor of Lycandos. The Strategist quickly found reasons to delay the Alesis' trip and then, using the excuse that the coast was too dangerous, kept Ana by his side and sent the others away by land. The voyage would have proven too arduous for the young woman. Ana accepted these measures with delight since she already felt toward the Illyrian the love and profound loyalty she would show him the rest of her life. Upon arriving in Byzantium, young Alesi complained to the Empress about Alar's behaviour. Irene intervened through Andronicus and admonished the Strategist, demanding the immediate return of Ana. Alar wrote his brother a letter, also kept in the archives of the Council, which throws plenty of light on his story and the reasons that kept him and Ana together. This is what he says:

"As far as Ana is concerned, I wish to explain what happened so that you may convey it to the Augusta in exactly the same terms. I feel too much devotion and loyalty towards our Empress to allow her, surrounded as she is by so many traitors and conspirators, to point her anger precisely at me.

"Ana is the only thing that now ties me to this world. Were it not for her I would have left my bones behind in some dark ambush long ago. You know this better than anyone and you also understand my reasons. In the beginning, when I barely knew her, I made her safety the pretext to keep her by my side. She slowly became more and more a part of my life, and today my world sustains itself through her skin, her fragrance, her words, her pleasant company in bed and the manner in which she understands me, thanks to her lovely clairvoyance, the truths and certainties I have conquered in my withdrawal from the world and its sordid, courtly fallacies. Thanks to her I have finally succeeded in capturing a truth sufficient for me to live out each day: the truth of her warm body, the truth of her soft loyal voice, the truth in her astonished large eyes. Because my case bears such close resemblance to that of an adolescent in love, it is quite probable that those in the court will not understand. However, I know the Augusta will accept the reasons behind the particular meaning of my conduct. She has known me for many years and, hidden behind her current Christian soul, lies the sharp Athenian who was once my loyal friend and protector.

"Because I know how fragile, how weak, any human attempt can be at preserving a relationship, like mine with Ana, against everything and everyone, if the Despoena insists on her returning to Constantinople, I will not lift a finger to prevent it. But there will end all interest of mine in continuing to serve the one who so clumsily hurts me."

Andronicus conveyed his brother's answer to Irene. The Empress was moved by the Illyrian's words and promised to drop the matter. Ana remained by Alar's side for two years and travelled with him to cities and posts that bordered the Empire, resting during the summer in a hidden port on the coast where a Venetian friend had given the Strategist a small house. But the

Alesis did not give up and, at a certain point, when Irene needed to negotiate a loan with some Genoese merchants, the family backed the debt with its signature. The Basilissa was forced to intervene, however unwillingly, in a definitive manner by ordering the return of Ana. The couple received Irene's messenger and conferred with him through the night. The next day, Ana the Cretan set sail for Constantinople and Alar went back to the capital of his province. Those present could not but be struck by the serenity with which they said goodbye to each other. They all knew the Strategist's profound attachment to the young woman, the manner in which he made the smallest aspect of his life depend on her. His intimate friends, however, were not surprised by the Illyrian's calm: they understood his way of thinking very well. They knew that a lucid, deeply rooted fatalism made him seem indifferent at critical times.

Alar never mentioned the Cretan's name again. He kept with him a few of her objects and some letters she had written to him once, while he was away taking charge of provisions and military preparations of the fleet anchored in Malta. He also kept an earring that the young woman had forgotten in their bed the first night they spent together at the fortress of St. Stephen of Damascus.

One day, he called his officers for an audience. The Strategist conveyed his intentions to them with the following words:

"Ahmid Kabil has gathered his army and is preparing an unprecedented incursion into our provinces. This time, though he does not count on the Emir's full backing, he can rely on his vigilant impartiality. If we go into Syria by surprise and get Kabil at his headquarters, where he is currently preparing his troops, victory will surely be ours. Once we are finished with him, the Emir will violate his neutrality and will throw himself against us, knowing that we are far from our headquarters, unable to procure help. My plan consists of asking for reinforcements from Byzantium and bringing them here in secret, to strengthen the citadels along the border, where half our troops will be lodged.

"Once the Emir is done with us — and it would be sheer madness to expect otherwise, since the battle will be fought fifty to one — he will turn his attention to the borders, only to meet a far more powerful resistance than he suspects. At that moment, he will be the one far away from his headquarters. Our men will surround him there and cut off his retreat.

"We will have thus eliminated two powerful enemies of the Empire by sacrificing a handful of our men. I will be going against the rules this time, and will not be the one designating the commanders and soldiers who should remain, and who should go into enemy territory with me. You are free to choose. Tomorrow at dawn you may convey your decision to me. I want you to be sure of one thing: those of you who decide to go with me to defeat Kabil, have no possibility of coming back alive. The Emir will be watching out for the slightest mistake on our part and he will want to take relentless advantage of this unique opportunity. Those who decide to stay behind to join the reinforcements we have requested from our Despoena, will form up to the left; those who decide to go with me, will form on the right side. That is all."

It is said that the loyalty his people bore Alar was such that the officers decided to draw lots among themselves to determine who would stay and who would go with the Strategist, as not one of them wished to desert him. Next morning, Alar inspected his army and lectured those who would be staying, calling on them to defend the borders of the Empire. His words were greeted with tears by many. The troops who had chosen to go with him into the desert were ordered to assemble somewhere in the Mardaites of Syria. Two weeks later, close to forty thousand soldiers joined the Illyrian there and under his personal command, marched into the arid mountains of Asia Minor.

Alar's campaign is described in scrupulous detail by Alexius Comnenus in his *Military Accounts*, an invaluable document for learning about military life at the time and understanding the causes which would lead to the destruction of the Empire by the Turks centuries later. Alar had not been mistaken. Once the slippery Ahmid Kabil had been defeated, with minimal losses to Greek lines, he retreated to his Theme. Half-way down the road, his column was forced to make a retreat and was caught by an avalanche of janissaries and the Turkish infantry, who stuck to his heels without letting go of their prey. With the intention of avoiding the complete annihilation of the regiments that had gone into Syria, Alar had divided his troops into three groups which fanned out toward different parts of Byzantine territory. Believing that this was the bulk of the army, the Turks fell into the trap and clung to the column at the extreme left, which was under the command of the Strategist. Hounded day and night by an evergrowing mass of Muslims, Alar ordered that they stop at the Oasis of Kazheb to confront the enemy there. They formed into a square as was the Byzantine tradition. The Turks began their siege and, as the remaining columns retreated intact into the Empire to go and join the defenders at the advanced posts, Alar's men were being felled by Muslim arrows. On the fourth day of the siege, Alar decided to try to exit at night and attack the besiegers from the rearguard. The possibility existed of frightening them away by making them believe that these were reinforcements from Lycandos. He gathered the Macedonians and two Bulgarian regiments and consulted them regarding his plan. They accepted peacefully and at midnight slipped away, down the cool sands that stretched out into the horizon. Without alerting the Turks, they crossed their lines, hid in an incline and waited for dawn to come. Unfortunately for the Greeks, the bulk of the Emir's troops marched into the battleground that morning. At the crack of dawn a rain of arrows announced the men's end. A vast swell of infantry and janissaries spread over the surrounding incline. They never had a chance to fight the Turks hand-to-hand, so impenetrable was the barrier of arrows coming from the enemy. The Macedonians attacked in a frenzy and were annihilated in a few minutes by the janissaries' scimitars. A few Hungarians, plus the Strategist's private guard, surrounded Alar as he impassively watched the slaughter.

The first arrow pierced him through the back and came out of his chest level with his top rib. Before completely losing all his strength, he aimed at a mahdi who was amusing himself by killing Bulgarians with a bow from the top of his horse. Alar threw his sword, and rammed it into him. A second arrow pierced Alar through the throat. He began to lose blood very quickly now and, wrapping himself in his cape, he threw himself to the ground with a vague smile on his face. As they fought their enemy, the Bulgarian fanatics sang religious hymns and psalms in praise of Christ, with the blind and feverish faith of the newly converted. Surrounded by the monotonous voices of these martyrs, death began coming to the Strategist.

A joyous confirmation of all his reasons for being suddenly came to him. In truth, the moment we are born we are condemned to fall into a trap with no exit. The efforts of reason, religion's specious net, man's weak and transitory faith in the powers he invents, or in those which are foreign to him, history's awkward progress, political convictions, the Greek and Roman systems of government, all these suddenly appeared as foolish child's play to Alar. Faced with the emptiness that was overwhelming him with the same speed as his blood left him, he searched for a reason for having lived, something that could validate the acceptance of this nothingness, and suddenly, like a fresh rush of blood, the memory of Ana the Cretan began to fill his entire life on earth with meaning. The delicate blue weave of her veins under her white breasts, the way her pupils opened with surprise and tenderness, the way she clung to his skin as he watched her sleep, their combined gasping, their breathing night after night like a sea eternally palpitating, her assured white hands, her firm fingers and almond-shaped nails, the way she listened, her gait. The memory of each one of her words rose to tell the Strategist that his life had not been in vain, that there is nothing one can ask for, other than the secret harmony that unites us fleetingly with the great mystery of the other, allowing us to walk part of the way in her company. The unity brought about by the lasting memory of her body, the solitary scream of the one seeking to communicate with the other, albeit imperfectly and vaguely, these were suddenly enough for him to go on to death with that enormous joy now beginning to confuse itself with the blood gushing out of his heart. A final arrow nailed him to the ground as it pierced his chest. But by that point he was already prey to the disorderly, fleeting happiness of someone who knows himself to be the owner of the illusory emptiness of death.

Translator's Afterword

I first read *The Mansion* shortly after it appeared in the form it takes in this translation (1973), at the urging of Ludwig Zeller, to whom I owe my literary education and the example of the writing life. I read it with fervour, egged on by its lushness, its drama, its sensual power. It made a profound impression on me. Over the years the images of La Machiche, Don Graci, Simón Bolívar and Alar the Byzantine strategist would come back, meshing with my own sensations and experiences of life.

Meeting Álvaro Mutis in person in 1987 no doubt inspired me to undertake the translation of this work. His presence, his voice, the sweep of his gestures, held the immediate recognition of the stories read years earlier. In that identification lay a feeling of complicity with my own imagination. Those newfound emotions enriched the translation experience as it progressed from revision to revision, and the manuscript made its way from one publisher to another, until finding its home with Ekstasis Editions.

The Mansion is Mutis's first book of fiction. It is a youthful work, and it is strong because it is born of the one experience that marked him as a person and as a writer. Sometime in the 1950's Mutis was unjustly jailed in Lecumberri, the infamous Mexico City prison. Out of that experience came his prison diaries *Diario de Lecumberri*, a work which forms the basis for most of the stories in *The Mansion*. Except for the title novella, which was written with a view to adaptation for the cinema by his friend Luis Buñuel, one recognizes many of the men Mutis got to know while in prison. Their daily confrontations with life *in extremis*, their struggle to rise above the injustices and humiliations they were subjected to, strongly inform the characters of the book at hand. More than any experience prior to or since, Álvaro Mutis's one year imprisonment defined the general feeling of entrapment in reality and existential fatalism that accosts Don Graci in the title tale, the fisherman Peter in "Before the Cock Crows," Simón Bolívar in "The Last Face," Sharaya in the story by the same name, and Alar in "The Strategist's Death."

Perhaps more than Mutis's prison experience, the title novella "The Mansion of Araucaíma" finds its roots in the author's origins, his childhood spent in Jesuit schools in Belgium, and in the plantation his family once owned, situated in *tierra caliente*, a concept which, both in the author's and in my opinion, is untranslatable. At once hot and lush, but neither desert-like nor tropical, the climate of *tierra caliente* carries with it moments of lassitude and ennui, and also of vigor and relief, especially when it rains. I tried to translate the subtitle of the title story, *Relato gótico de tierra caliente*, using various adjectives, including "lush" and "sultry," but ultimately settled for a literal translation, however unsatisfactory: *Gothic Tale of the Tropics*. Where proper names are concerned, I felt that they should retain their Spanish spellings, as many are inventions of the author's, like "Araucaíma," and "Machiche."

In the tradition of other Latin American fiction writers, Mutis makes excellent use of the apocryphal. For example, while two of the stories are set in specific historical periods, there is a deliberate attempt to subvert history in order to maintain a strictly fictional universe. For example, Mutis has stated that in "The Strategist's Death" he combined and mixed up the events that characterized the reigns of the two Irenes: both were Empresses of

Byzantium though in reality they lived several hundred years apart. The same applies to Simón Bolívar. More than a historical portrait of the Latin American hero, what drives Mutis's story is the metaphorical possibilities this figure offers the writer and, by extension, the reader of "The Last Face."

I feel that translation is a form of writing vicariously, akin to putting on the original author's clothes and adapting them to one's body and soul. In the process, the translator absorbs the lessons, anxieties, emotions explored by the other, the original author. Translation is the deepest reading one can do of a work of literature. This probably explains why translating the title story brought back memories and echoes of the first time I read it, long ago, while still in my teens. Translating "Before the Cock Crows," on the other hand, often proved emotionally difficult because the story so graphically and effectively portrays violence: Mutis's contemporary rendition of Christ's *via crucis* is, in my view, a powerful metaphor of the endemic violence that has gripped Colombia for the last one hundred years. By the time I translated "The Last Face," Gabriel García Márquez had published *The General in his Labyrinth*, a novel based on the life of Bolívar which was inspired by the very story I was translating. The overall sensation was one of working with the stuff of literary legend. One of the happiest experiences in my career as a translator was that of rendering the story "The Strategist's Death" into English. Not only is this one of the most beautiful works of fiction I have ever read, translating it fortuitously coincided with a trip I had just made to Turkey where I visited the Roman ruins of Ephesus, traveled the Aegean Coast and explored Istanbul, or, more exactly for Mutis's purposes, Constantinople. Once I sat down to translate the Mutis's story, therefore, I understood the geography and cultural context of "The Strategist's Death" and, further, the protagonist's conclusion that man's effort to bring rational order to the world is an adventure fraught with danger and, sometimes, even futility.

Translating *The Mansion* has, as Mutis himself expresses in the last story of this collection, filled me with "enormous joy... fleeting happiness" and for this I thank him.

Toronto, January 2004.